The Lance of Longinus

John Conlee

Pale Horse Books

ISBN: 978-1-939917-36-2

Cover Design: Sally Stiles

Also by John Conlee:

THE DRAGON STONE

A CUP OF KINDNESS

THE KING OF MUD & GRASS

IN THE SUMMER COUNTRY

THE HEATER

ROUNDING THIRD

THE VOYAGE OF MAELDUN

THE BROTHERS PENDRAGON

THE LAST PENDRAGON

CATACLYSM

THE CHAUCER CODEX

Available at: www.PaleHorseBooks.com
Also at Amazon and Barnes & Noble

The Lance of Longinus

❖ ❖ ❖

John Conlee

❖ ❖

But one of the soldiers with a spear pierced his side, and forthwith came there out blood and water.

— The Gospel of St. John, 19:34

The soldiers gave him vinegar and gall, offered it to him to drink. "If thou art the king of the Jews, deliver thyself," they said.

Then Longinus, a certain Roman soldier, took a spear and pierced his side. And presently there came forth blood and water.

— The Gospel of Nichodemus, 7:7-8
(non-canonical)

. . . a squire came forth from a chamber carrying a white lance by the middle of its shaft, a drop of blood issuing from its tip and flowing down to the squire's hand . . . .

Perceval swore he would not spend two nights in the same lodging until he had . . . found the bleeding lance and learned the true reason why it bleeds.

— Chretien de Troyes, **Le Conte du Graal**
(The Story of the Grail)

❖ ❖

❖ ❖

Prologue

Allie, Eva, Charles, and Professor Wentworth stare down at the body lying on the flagstones of the small dark chapel. The man's arms extend from his torso at 90-degree angles; his legs, stretched out straight, are crossed at the ankles. His hands have been turned palms upward. At the center of his palms are small bloody puncture wounds; they look like stigmata. A single puncture wound is visible in his top ankle. His bottom ankle, which isn't visible, presumably has one too. On the right side of his chest, his torn and blood-soaked dress shirt displays a large stab wound.

"Oh, my Lord!" Eva moans, "the man's been crucified.*"*

"Yes, after a fashion," the professor replies, "though at the moment he is sans cross, spikes, and crown of thorns. I wonder what could have happened to the spikes. Strange, that. Did he, she, or they take them away? Why would they? The spear I think we can account for," he says, glancing over at the glass-fronted display case, its door not fully secured.

"Does anyone know who this man is?" the professor asks.

After just a brief pause Charles says, "Yes, I believe I do."

❖ ❖

Glastonbury

CHAPTER 1
— The Tor —

Charles Bascombe, having an hour to kill before the hotel's three p.m. check-in time, leaves his small suitcase with the desk clerk at The Pilgrims' Inn. Then, slinging his backpack over his shoulder, he sets off along the streets of Glastonbury. The interval before checking in gives him a perfect opportunity for a quick visit to the famous, enigmatic hill known as the Glastonbury Tor. It's something he's long wanted to do but never had the chance before today.

Charles strides casually up the busy High Street and threads his way through a bevy of shoppers and tourists. On his left he takes note of the Church of St. John the Baptist with its soaring 15th-century tower. He knows that's where the Holy Grail Conference will take place beginning tonight. On the right side of the busy street he takes in the names of a variety of small shops and boutiques. They reveal to him that Glastonbury is not your usual, run-of-the-mill English town. At the T-intersection at the top of the High, Charles turns right onto a quieter residential street, and then steps up his pace. The desk clerk told him that it's about a fifteen-minute walk to the foot of the Tor, which is a couple hundred yards beyond the entrance to the grounds of Chalice Well. As he passes Chalice Well, Charles remembers that a cocktail party is scheduled to be held there tomorrow evening.

When he reaches the base of the Tor, he stops and takes in the sight. He sees that several other visitors are now winding their way up the steep, undulating pathway toward the summit of this unusual hill, the top of which is crowned by the impressive Tower of St. Michael. The tower is all that remains of the medieval church that once stood there.

Charles has seen many photos of the Tor, but it's even more impressive in person than in the photos. The Tor itself, he knows, is a natural phenomenon that rises dramatically above the low-lying Somerset Levels; along its left side is some odd terracing that was presumably shaped long, long ago by the hands of men—shaped for some unknown but often speculated about purpose or purposes. Charles pops the lens cover off his camera and takes a couple of photos. The white, puffy clouds scudding across the blue, mid-April sky, he hopes, will provide a striking backdrop.

Five minutes later Charles has mounted the steep hill. Despite the fact that he is quite fit, he still needs a moment to catch his breath. He stands to one side of the flattish area at the top of the Tor, an area that extends some thirty yards beyond the tower and maybe fifteen yards in front of it and on each side. A heterogeneous array of visitors mills about on the open grassy areas, including a group of schoolboys, two families with small children, and several bizarrely attired young men and women in semi-medieval dress with flowing robes and colorful capes. Charles guesses that Glastonbury New-Agers comprise this last group. The town, with all its mystical associations, had long been a haven for them. Despite himself, Charles can't help but smile at the sight of the New-Agers and their intentionally outlandish attire. They make quite a contrast to the schoolboys, all dressed alike in their white shirts and dark trousers. Whatever floats your boat, he thinks. Charles also notices a pair of middle-aged men attired in tweed sportcoats and wearing English flat-caps. Fellow academics, he guesses, also in Glastonbury to attend the Holy Grail conference.

A young couple huddles in the lee of St. Michael's Tower, shielding themselves from the stiff spring breezes. Just in front of the tower the schoolboys are gathered about their teacher who is lecturing to them about the Tor. A few of the boys, who are probably about eleven or twelve, are taking notes. Charles moves closer to listen in.

"All this low green land you see around us," the teacher says, "is known as the Somerset Levels. Before this area was drained late in the Middle Ages, most of it was under water. Look closely and you can make out a lot of the drainage ditches. Back then the Tor was virtually an island. Some people believe that this hill was once known as The Isle of Avalon. Back then, some folks even believed it to be the entrance to the Celtic Faerie Otherworld.

"Christian churches have been built here since Anglo-Saxon times. All that remains of the last of them is this tower. Does anybody know to whom it is dedicated?"

"St. Michael the Archangel, the warrior angel who did battle with Satan," a boy quickly pipes up.

"Quite right, Peter. As you may know, there are many high places in Europe dedicated to St. Michael."

"Like Mont Saint-Michel in France," says another boy.

"Quite right, Dicky."

"My parents took me there," says the boy named Dicky. "It's really cool."

"One of the last of the medieval churches to be built here," the teacher continues, "was actually destroyed by an earthquake. Maybe those ancient pagan gods of the Celts were getting a little of their own back? The very last church was torn down during what's known as the Dissolution of the Monasteries. Does anyone know who did that?"

"Henry VIII?"

"Quite right again, Peter. To be more precise, it was actually Thomas Cromwell, Henry VIII's notorious henchman."

"Sir," the boy asks his teacher, "that small stone carving on the front of the tower? What's that all about? It looks like a woman milking a cow." Some of the other boys giggle.

"I don't actually know, Peter. But yes, that is what it looks like."

Charles, who's been following all of this with genuine interest, can't keep himself from chiming in. "I believe it's a depiction of St. Brigid," he says, loud enough for the teacher and the boys to hear. "According to some historians, she came from Ireland and spent a few years in this area. The image of the cow probably reflects her close association with domestic animals and with lactation."

"Ah, yes," the young teacher says, nodding his head. "I believe you are right. Well, thank you for that."

"Sorry to have intruded," Charles says sheepishly.

"Quite all right, sir. Peter here has a great deal of curiosity. It's nice to have one of his questions answered."

"Would you mind if I asked a question?" Charles says.

"Not at all. And if I can't answer it, Peter or Dicky probably can." A few of the other boys giggle.

"I believe there's another hill near Glastonbury called Wearyall Hill. Can we see it from here?"

"Ah. The one where Joseph of Arimathea plunged his staff into the earth and it grew into the Glastonbury Thorn. Well, yes, we can just make it out from here. It's over there to the southwest," he says, pointing. "It rises up just beyond the rooftops of the town. Do you see it?"

"Okay, yes, I do see it."

"It's only a five-minute walk from the entrance to the Abbey. Quite worth it, actually, though the poor thorn itself has been horribly desecrated."

The teacher glances at his watch. "All right, then, lads, time we headed back to the coach."

"Sir," the boy named Peter says to Charles as the other boys scamper off, "are you an American?"

"I am. I've been in Oxford doing research."

"In Oxford? Goodness. How I envy you, sir. Well, thank you for telling us about St. Brigid. I'll do some research about her."

"An excellent idea, Peter. All the best of luck to you."

"And to you, sir." The boy hurries off to catch up with his school group.

The afternoon has grown chilly, and only a few people remain on the top of the Tor. Charles takes a last look at the tower, then steps to the path that leads back down the steep hill.

Walking just ahead of him Charles notices the pair of flat-capped men whom he suspects are fellow academics. As he strolls slowly back to the center of town, he remains thirty yards behind the two men, who, as it turns out, are also staying at the Pilgrims' Inn, along with a great many of the other conference attendees.

Indeed, Charles is correct in thinking that the two men he'd followed back to the hotel from the Tor were scholars who'd come for the conference on the Holy Grail. Their names are George Harpole and Geoff Rawlinson, and they are medievalists from the University of Hull in Yorkshire. Like Charles, they've come to Glastonbury to attend the conference. But they've also come for another purpose, one that holds the prospect of making them quite wealthy men. That is, it holds the prospect of making them quite wealthy men if it doesn't end up getting them killed.

❖

The small coach carrying the group of schoolboys is now on its way back to the village in Dorsetshire where their boarding school is located. The boys fill the coach with their noisy chatter, though a couple of them are trying to read and one or two are engrossed in the games they're playing on hand-held devices. Peter, the youth with whom Charles had spoken atop the Tor, swivels his head to take a final glimpse back through the coach window at the intriguing hill. It astonishes him that you can still see the Tor from such a distance, maybe fifteen miles or more. Even now it's a dramatic sight.

The day in Glastonbury has enthralled the boy. So much so, in fact, that now a plan begins to take shape in his mind. Tomorrow is Friday, and then the boys will have a totally free weekend. This isn't a parents' weekend or a games weekend, and while some of the boys will be going home to spend the weekend with their families, Peter isn't one of them. How about if I return to Glastonbury and check out some of the other wonders I missed seeing on the school trip? he thinks. It would probably be just a forty-five-minute bus ride. He could check the bus schedule and see if there's an early morning one that will get him to Glastonbury and then an early evening one that will get him back.

Peter finds the idea of spending a whole day in Glastonbury on his own very exciting. He decides not to share his plan with anyone, not even Dickie, his best chum. This will be his own private adventure.

CHAPTER 2
— An Oxford Bluestocking —

Back at the hotel, Charles only needs a few moments to unpack his small suitcase and get settled in his room. Then he sprawls out on the double bed. He has a couple of hours before tonight's introductory session, so he intends to read for a bit and then grab a quick bite before heading over to St. John's Church. Alwyn Tremayne, his friend who is driving up from Cornwall to spend the weekend with him, isn't likely to arrive before ten, and that's assuming she gets away from the art gallery where she works in St. Ives, by around six.

It's been nearly a month and a half since Charles has seen Allie, longer than he likes. They've known each other for less than a year, but in that time she's become very dear to Charles. But he, like her, prefers taking things slowly in their developing relationship. She's told him she's read that Capricorns, her sign, and Virgos, his sign, make a good combination, both being earth signs, though neither of them puts any real stock in such nonsense.

Charles stretches his long legs out on the bed and settles in to read another couple chapters of P.D. James' *The Black Tower*. He's been working his way through her mystery novels, which he finds intelligent and thought-provoking, if not exhilarating or captivating. Charles does feel an affinity with Adam Dalgliesh, her detective, who, like Charles, is what's called a high-functioning introvert.

At 6:45, Charles wanders into the vestibule of the Church of St. John and steps up to the long table behind which sit a trio of be-spectacled and be-cardiganed middle-aged women.

"Your name, please?" the first woman asks him.

"Charles Bascombe."

"Bascombe, then you'll be in my box—A to H. Bascombe, Bascombe," she says to herself, riffling quickly through the plastic name-holders. "Ah, here you are. One of our American guests, I see."

"Yes, that's right."

"Going to be quite a few of you here. Well, it's very nice to have you." She makes a tick mark beside his name on her printed sheets.

"Thank you," he says. "I'm looking forward to the talks."

"We think it's rather a good lineup. Oh, and you'll notice that we didn't put your academic affiliation on the name badge. More than half the attendees aren't academics, so we thought it best to be egalitarian and just use people's names."

"Makes sense to me," Charles says. Charles is anything if not egalitarian.

"Take a seat wherever you like in the nave. Mr. Bright-Rogers will be offering the welcoming remarks in about twenty minutes."

"Thanks again," Charles says. He clips the name badge onto

his shirt pocket and helps himself to a printed program from a stack of them on a small table by the doorway. Then he passes on into the nave. Quite a few people have already taken their seats, mostly on the right-hand side of the central aisle, so Charles, as is his wont, chooses the left. He walks over to the far aisle, then goes about halfway up the nave before turning into an empty row; he selects a seat about a third of the way in. He likes having plenty of elbowroom, and he's never been fond of having to make small talk with strangers.

Charles takes a moment to look about him at the assemblage of folks who have gathered here in this cathedral-like church for the conference's initial session. It's a curious-looking group. He's been forewarned by his mentor, Professor William Wentworth, that anything concerning the Holy Grail inevitably attracts a wide assortment of folks, including not a few wackos and weirdoes, along with some would-be treasure hunters. But Charles knows for certain some quite serious and well-known scholars will be here, including a few famous archeologists and antiquarians.

Of course, at the moment Charles can only judge these people by their physical appearances and their wearing apparel, but those things alone tell him that this conference will be rather different from the other academic conferences he's previously attended in the U.S. and U.K. Looking at those already in their seats, he estimates that there are probably between 75 and 100 people present and that nearly half of them are women. Some of the women, Charles sees with a smile, belong to what the professor rather snidely refers to as "the blue-rinse brigade."

For the next few minutes Charles sits quietly and glances through the program he picked up near the entrance. It lists the various sessions scheduled for the next two and a half days of the conference. After a brief perusal of the offerings, Charles feels sure he's in for an amusing time, even if most of the talks don't portend great intellectual enlightenment. But there are a couple of sessions, he's relieved to see, that will focus on aspects of the Grail Legend as portrayed in medieval literature, both European and British. These talks will certainly be of interest to him. After his cursory examination of the program, he places it down on the seat to his left in the hope that it will ensure the seat remains empty, should other people come crowding into his row.

Tonight's opening session is really just a chance for the hosts to welcome the early arrivers, and for people who are already there to say hello to one another. As Charles looks about him, he sees no one right off that he knows—though he does spot the two flat-capped men he'd noticed earlier in the afternoon up on the Tor, now minus their caps.

More people trickle in, and now more of them take seats on his side of the nave. Now someone even has the temerity to enter his row. Charles casts a quick glance to his left and sees a tall, slender, dark-haired woman making her way towards him. To his relief, she stops and sits down with three seats still separating them. Noticing him glance her way, she says, "You don't mind if I sit here, do you?"

"No," Charles replies, "please do."

"Excuse me again," she says, "but would you mind if I had

a quick peek at your program? I'm afraid I neglected to collect one when I came in."

"Certainly," Charles says. "Here you go." He picks it up off the seat next to him and hands it to her.

"Oh, thank you so much," she says. "By the way, I'm Evangeline. Evangeline Brooksby."

"Hello," Charles says. "I'm Charles Bascombe. Nice to make your acquaintance."

The woman spends the next five minutes reading through Charles' program. Then, still holding it, she exclaims, just loud enough for Charles to hear, "Oh, dear, here we go again. 'The Chalice and the Bleeding Lance: An Anthropological Interpretation.' Not that tired old razzmatazz again. 'An Anthropological Interpretation' indeed. Martin Nicholson, the silly little man, has sex on the brain."

Charles, slightly taken aback by her blunt words, glances over at her and says, "Maybe he'll surprise you and have something fresh to say. One can always hope."

"Well, at least it should give some of these old biddies a thrill, sexing things up a bit."

"Ha, ha," Charles laughs. "I take it you know Mr. Nicholson?"

"As it happens, I do. Well, not really *know* know. But I've met the old lecher a few times at Oxford cocktail parties. After a few gins, he can get rather free with his hands."

Charles hasn't yet had a really good look at this young woman named Evangeline Brooksby, but he knows it would take more than a few gins for him to want to paw most of the Oxford blue stockings he's come in contact with during his year in the U.K.

"Excuse me," she says again. "I've just realized who you are. You're Charles Bascombe, the Chaucer scholar. Isn't that right?"

"Well, umm, yes, I guess I am."

"Sorry, took a minute for the penny to drop. You wrote that brilliant monograph on 'The Book of the Lion'."

Charles nods. "I'm not sure that 'brilliant' is quite the right word. 'Controversial,' certainly."

"It's kicked up quite a fuss, that's for sure. So, you're interested in the Grail Legends as well?"

"Well, yes and no," Charles admitted. "They aren't a burning scholarly interest of mine, but I do enjoy teaching Malory and Chretien de Troyes, both of whose works I admire a great deal. Being here is mostly just an excuse to have a few days away from Oxford. How about you?"

"Well, in fact, the Grail Legends happen to be the subject of my doctoral dissertation. I'm currently at St. Catherine's, teaching a tutorial on them. It's just a temporary appointment, alas, but one never knows what may materialize. As you say, one can always hope."

"Well, good luck," Charles said.

The rector of St. John's Church speaks first, welcoming everyone and saying how pleased he is for the church to host the conference. Then he quickly turns things over to Nigel Bright-Rogers, the conference's director, for his opening remarks. Charles finds Bright-Rogers' remarks polished and witty, if mostly predictable and perfunctory. But the man does cause a bit of a stir when he closes with a teaser: "In addition to a most enlightening set of sessions and panels, we have a rather special surprise for you this weekend—something we are very, very pleased to be able to make available to you. No, we haven't got the Holy Grail itself (polite laughter), but perhaps we have the next best thing. Well, sort of we do. And that, I think, is the note on which we should leave things this evening.

"Now, I hope that all of you will stay on for a bit to chat informally, introduce yourselves to others whom you may not already know, and of course have a glass of wine. Coffee and Danishes will be available in the morning on tables at the back of the nave, beginning at 9. The first plenary address will be here in the nave at 10. Informal lunch at 1. Drinks Party at Chalice Well at 5, following the afternoon sessions. So, enjoy."

Charles does not stay on to chat informally. He exits the church straight away and strolls the short distance back down High Street to the hotel. It isn't nine o'clock yet, and it's likely to be at least another hour before Allie arrives, but he wants to be there when she does. It's been a long six weeks since they've spent some time together, and he's excited to see her.

In his room, Charles notices the message light flashing on his room phone. It turns out to be a message from Allie, who, she says, just covering all her bases, since she knows Charles rarely checks his mobile phone for messages. She says she's been held up at the gallery by a last-minute customer and probably won't arrive until about eleven. So, not being in a reading mood, Charles decides to wander down and see what might be doing in the hotel lounge.

Only a few guests are in the lounge—a youngish couple huddled near the TV, an older woman sitting and knitting in a far corner, and two elderly chaps playing cards. Charles notices the cribbage board on the table beside them. He settles himself in a wing chair not far from the card players and listens to their banter.

"Fifteen-two, fifteen-four, fifteen-six, run of three makes nine, pair makes eleven," says one of them; then he lifts his back peg and moves it eleven spaces in front of his other peg.

"I've just a measly double run for eight," says the other man. "Well, let's see what wonders my crib may offer, eh?" As it turns out, only four points. "Ah," the man declares, spotting the jack in his crib, "and his knobs! Almost makes it worthwhile." He moves his peg thirteen spaces, putting him slightly ahead. Glancing at the board, Charles reckons that the next hand should resolve matters, one way or another. It'll be a tight finish, for sure.

Two more men enter the lounge, each carrying a full pint of beer. They stand just inside the door for a moment and study the others scattered about the room, then head for a sofa against a wall close to the TV. After a second Charles realizes they're the pair of men he'd seen earlier atop the Tor and then again just a bit ago at the introductory session of the conference. They still wear their tweed jackets but not their flat caps. He wonders if they might be two of the speakers. As he observes them his intuition tells him that, despite being close friends or perhaps colleagues, there's some tension between them. It's just a feeling he has, probably arising from the men's body language more than anything else. They seat themselves on opposite ends of the sofa, and although Charles can't make out their words, they seem less chummy now than they had up on the Tor.

At 10:45, Charles pulls his phone from his pocket and sees he's received a recent message: "There in fifteen minutes." It was sent at 10:40, so Charles quickly types a reply. "Our room is 109. Up the central stairs, along the hallway to the left." It's a first-floor room, which to Charles means a second-floor room, a simple distinction he's still not used to, even after nearly a year in the U.K.

As he readies himself to leave the lounge, Charles overhears a bit of animated conversation that now emanates from the pair of academics he's been observing.

"No! You must not do that!"

"Don't tell me what I must or must not do."

"Geoff, it could be a matter of life or death."

"Not my life or death. Maybe yours—though I should be so lucky."

"Yes, Geoff—maybe mine."

The men get to their feet and walk toward the lounge door. Their voices are lower now, and Charles doesn't catch their last words.

Had their words been audible to Charles, this is what he would have heard.

"George," Geoff says, "it's you who got her killed. And it's you who's likely to share her fate."

"That's not entirely fair, Geoff."

"Not fair? Ha. When a quarter of a million quid comes through the door, George, fair flies out the window."

CHAPTER 3
— The Dolorous Stroke —

Allie and Charles are starting on their scrambled eggs on toast when Professor William Wentworth pulls out an empty chair at the end of their table and lowers himself onto it.

"Professor!" Allie exclaims. "What an unexpected pleasure. Charlie didn't say you were coming. When did you get here, sir?"

"Ten minutes ago, Ms. Tremayne. Charlie didn't tell you I was coming because he didn't know it. Nor did I, in fact, until about half five this morning. Mind if I help myself to a splash of coffee?" He was already pouring it from the coffee urn into an empty cup. "So, Charles, it appears you had an ulterior motive for wanting to come to this god-awful conference, eh?" He glances at Allie and smiles. "I kind of suspected it might be something along those lines."

"He just wanted to experience all the wonders of Glastonbury, sir," Allie says, "the abbey, the Tor, Chalice Well, Wearyall Hill, the Holy Thorn."

"Ah yes, of course he did. And, I would suggest, my dear, that isn't all. But, oh my, who can blame the lad?" He beams a warm smile at her.

"Certainly didn't expect to see you here, Professor," Charles says, "a man who never tires of scoffing at the Grail legends. Had a change of heart?"

"No, Charlie, no change of heart. And yes, they're most assuredly 'not my thing,' as my old Berkeley chums might've said back in the late '60s. But Charlie, I can't allow you and Allie to have all the fun without me. I'm rather hurt that you decided to leave me off the team. I'm part of it too, you know."

"Team? I didn't know we were a team, sir," Charles said.

"We most assuredly are, Charlie. Say, you wouldn't mind if I just helped myself to a slice of your toast, would you? You seem to have quite a sufficiency. Oh, and maybe we could order up another pot of coffee? Yours seems suddenly depleted."

"Golly, I wonder why that is?"

"Oh, now Charlie. We shall need all the sustenance and fortification we can get, you know, before we brave the awfulness of what's lies before us this morning over there in the church."

"Well," Allie says, "I for one have been quite looking forward to this whole experience. There are some illustrious scholars on the program. And I'm sorry to have to say it, sir, but you've begun to sound rather like an academic snob—the very thing my father always hated so much about Oxford."

"Allie, me a snob?"

"Teetering on the verge, sir, definitely teetering. As for young Charles here, he's just an inverted snob."

"Hold on a second," Charles says, "leave me out of this."

"Ha, ha," the professor laughs. "Charlie, I think she's

got us pegged. Allie, speaking of your father, how's the old curmudgeon doing? Haven't heard from him in a good while."

"Very excited, sir. On Cloud Nine, actually. He is now the proud possessor of a first edition of Shakespeare's sonnets."

"Wow!" Charles says. "The 1609 quarto edition?" Allie nods. "That's fantastic! Only about a dozen of those in existence."

"Thirteen, actually," the professor says.

"And now, fourteen," Allie says. "This one sort of, umm, 'just happened to turn up.'"

"Oh, dear, not again," says the professor.

"Yes, again." All three of them laugh raucously, bringing them a variety of looks from the other breakfasters.

At 9:40, Allie, Charles and Professor Wentworth stroll up the High Street toward St. John's Church. Many people have already congregated outside the main entrance enjoying casual conversation, and the three of them have to thread their way carefully through the crowd in order to enter the vestibule. Allie and the professor join a short line of folks waiting to pick up their name badges. It's the third of the still be-spectacled, still be-cardiganed trio of women—rather like the Weird Sisters at the opening of *Macbeth*, Charles thinks—who have Allie's and the professor's badges.

"I'm William Wentworth," the professor says.

"Oh, yes, then you're one of mine—T to Zed." She fishes out his badge from the nearly empty box before her and puts a check mark by his name.

"Out of curiosity," the professor says, "in your batch, did

you, by any chance, have any names beginning with X?"

"Just the one."

"And what name would that be?"

"Well, I suppose it would be okay to tell you, since he's on the program. It's Dr. Xander. Dr. M. Xander. I can't tell what the M. stands for, because I don't know. I suspect it might be for Mohammed."

"Wouldn't surprise me in the least," the professor says. "It's the most common given name in the world, you know."

"Perhaps it is. But not in *this* part of the world," she says, almost as if she finds the matter distasteful.

"This is a very small part of the world," the professor says.

Ignoring his comment, the woman turns her attention to Allie. "And you, my dear?"

"Alwyn Tremayne."

"Here you are, dear. You wouldn't be the Cornish biblio-phile, by any chance?"

"No, sorry, that's not me. I'm the Cornish painter."

"Painter? Ah, yes, then I guess you've come especially for the session on the Grail Illustrations. Would that be right?"

"Oh yes, quite right," Allie replies, just to be agreeable. "And what time is that session?"

"It's this afternoon. Just check the program for the specific time and place."

"M. Xander," Charles murmurs as they pass on into the nave. "Kind of makes me think of Malcolm X."

"Well, you may be in the ballpark there, Charlie," the professor says. "I believe this chap is scheduled to give a talk titled, 'Islamic Influences on the Grail Legends'."

"Oh, yes, I saw it in the program."

"Well hello, Professor," says a tall, somewhat gaunt-looking woman who is standing by herself just inside the doorway.

"Eva," he replies cheerfully, "No surprise seeing you here. Let me introduce my friends."

"I've already met Charles," the woman says. "We introduced ourselves last evening." Her comment causes Allie's eyebrows to rise just barely perceptibly.

"Oh, yes, Evangeline, it's nice to see you again," Charles says gallantly. "This is my friend Alwyn." Allie reaches out a hand and the two women touch fingers briefly. Eva, Charles notices, is maybe two or three inches taller than Allie; not a beanpole exactly, though not nearly as shapely.

"Please do like the professor and call me Eva and not Evangeline. Can you imagine saddling a child with a four-syllable name? What kind of a parent does such a thing? Two or even three syllables aren't too many. But four? Four's more than a mouthful."

Allie nods. "I see your point. Eva it shall be," she says. "Well, perhaps we'd better find seats. Shall we get as close to the front as we can? I see some empty spaces up there in the fourth row." Eva, who without invitation has attached herself to the group, presses ahead and nabs the available seats for them.

As Charles follows in the wake of the others, he scans the rows of those already seated for familiar faces. To his surprise, the first ones he recognizes are the cribbage players from the night before. He hadn't had them down as being scholars, though maybe they aren't, since a lot of the folks here clearly aren't. The only other ones he recognizes are the two men he'd seen up on the Tor and then again last night in the hotel lounge, where they seemed to be having some sort of spat. He can't help wondering what that was all about.

Mr. Bright-Rogers raps on the lectern, bringing a swift hush to the chatter in the large and crowded space. He proceeds to offer a flowery welcome in his ringing, upper-class oratorical style; it's too self-indulgent and too long in Charles' opinion, but the man eventually gets around to introducing the speaker, Sorley MacPherson, a well-known art historian associated with a well-known museum in Manchester. Near the conclusion of Bright-Rogers' long-winded introduction, Professor Wentworth can be heard to mutter, not under his breath, "Give us a break, eh mate?" People sitting close by smile and a few chuckle audibly. Mr. Bright-Rogers either hasn't heard the remark, or he pretends he hasn't, but he does wrap things up at that point and turn the lectern over to the speaker.

Speaking with a hint of a Scottish burr, Mr. MacPherson announces that his subject will be the most famous artifact associated with the Grail legends after the Grail itself; it's the object known variously as the Holy Spear, the Spear of Destiny, or the Lance of Longinus. It's the weapon, he explains, used by a Roman soldier or centurion at the Crucifixion to pierce Christ's side. According to the *Gospel of John*, the only one of the four canonical gospels to preserve this detail, this is the spear that caused Christ's fifth and final wound while on the cross. The apocryphal *Gospel of Nicodemus* is the only work to provide the additional detail that the Roman was named Longinus.

"As the tradition developed and was elaborated upon during the Middle Ages," MacPherson says, "this holy artifact was desecrated when it was used to wound the Maimed King, also known as the Fisher King, an action sometimes called 'the dolorous stroke.' In Sir Thomas Malory's great Arthurian saga, it is Sir Balyn who strikes this blow, which incapacitates the king and brings about the Waste Land. Only a supremely Holy Grail Knight can undo this pair of catastrophes. Depending upon the specific work, that knight is Parsifal, Perceval, or Galahad."

The man's lecture, accompanied by PowerPoint illustrations, interests Charles a great deal. The several objects depicted in the illustrations include the Holy Lance that lies beneath the dome of St. Peter's Basilica in Rome; a spear kept in the Imperial Treasury in Vienna; a Holy Lance in a museum in Armenia; and yet another Holy Lance that was discovered in Antioch during the Crusades.

At the conclusion of the talk, MacPherson startles the audience by telling them that these objects are here in Glastonbury, and that they will be able to view them. His remark produces an audible gasp before the man sheepishly confesses that what he's just said isn't strictly true; the real objects aren't in fact here but rather some excellent reproductions. "You will be able to see these reproductions up close and personal, and photography is allowed. Mr. Bright-Rogers will explain to you how you can go about seeing them. Well, thank you very much for your kind attention."

The man receives a rousing round of applause, even from

Professor Wentworth.

"I'm afraid we've run over our time," Mr. Bright-Rogers says. "So sorry, but there won't be an opportunity just now for questions."

The professor makes an audible groan but refrains from saying what he's inclined to say.

"Let me just describe to you where and when we'll have the spears on view," Bright-Rogers adds. He does that briefly, then concludes by thanking the speaker once more (to more warm applause) and reminding everyone of the availability of boxed lunches. The afternoon panels, he said, will commence sharply at 2:15 in their assigned spaces.

"Sharply is good," the professor mutters, casting a disgusted look in Bright-Rogers' direction.

Leaving the professor contentedly in the Queen's Head Pub, Charles and Allie, carrying their box lunches, set off in search of Wearyall Hill. It's only a short walk from the center of town. The street that leads up the hill is steep but not long, and they soon push through the gate into the fenced area surrounding the hilltop. There before them stands the pathetic remains of the Glastonbury Thorn. Colorful ribbons and other tokens of love and affection bedeck the desecrated remains of the small tree.

"How horrible!" Allie declares. "Whoever did this despicable thing should be drawn and quartered!"

Charles shakes his head in dismay.

"I do hope they'll try to re-grow it with a fresh cutting from the tree at the Abbey," Allie says. "And then guard it really, really well."

"And maybe they could put in a well-concealed security camera," Charles says.

They move a little higher up the hill and find a comfortable grassy spot to sit and eat their lunches. As they eat, their eyes are inevitably drawn toward the Tor, a mile to the east.

"How wonderful," Charles says, quietly.

"Yes," Allie replies, "it is. And it's also wonderful to share a quiet moment alone with you. It's been too long, Charlie."

"It has," he says, squeezing her hand.

"Allie," he asks a moment later, "how many times have you been here?"

"To Glastonbury, four times, the first two with school groups. This is just my second time to climb Wearyall Hill." After a pause Allie says, "What do you think, Charlie? Could Joseph of Arimathea have really trod these hills 2,000 years ago? Did he see very nearly the same sight we're seeing? Did he really stab his staff into the earth on this hillside where it grew into the holy thorn?"

"I'd like to believe it," Charles says, "improbable as the legend is. However the thorn came to be here, it's still quite a wonder. It's a hawthorn but no ordinary one, for it blooms *twice* a year—in May, like all hawthorns—but then again at Christmas time."

"In honor of Christ's birth."

"That's what they say. A grand story," Charles says. "Joseph escaping from the Jews with the Grail in tow and bringing it here for safekeeping. A wondrous tale, whether or not it ever happened."

"So, it was Joseph who spirited the Grail away from the Holy Land and brought it to Britain?"

"Yes, according to the earliest stories in the Grail Tradition. In some versions Joseph of Arimathea was the first in a long succession of Grail Keepers, with Sir Galahad being the last."

"Charlie, what exactly *was* the Grail?"

"Good question. Most of the literary works aren't at all specific. A cup, a goblet, a chalice? A bowl, dish, or swallow plate? Was it used at the Last Supper? One thing agreed upon is that it was used to collect the blood from Christ's wounded side at the Crucifixion. In the literary works, few people ever get to see it. In Malory when it appears to the assembled Knights of the Round Table, it is completely covered by a cloth of "white samite" so none of the knights has a direct sight of it. The implication is that only the totally pure are permitted to have any contact with the Grail, even visually. When Lancelot tries enter the room where it's kept in Malory, his rash action causes him to be severely injured. Lancelot doesn't possess the innocence and purity of his son, Sir Galahad.

"The Grail and the Bleeding Lance are the holy of holies," Charles goes on. "When someone impure is brash enough to interact with them, he must pay a price. Sir Balyn, in Malory, as the speaker noted this morning, defiles the spear by using it to strike the Dolorous Stroke, and catastrophe ensues: the maiming of the King and the creation of the Waste Land. Only a pure Grail Knight can undo those events. The Maimed King,

Chretien de Troyes suggests, is sustained by the Grail and another vessel—vessels which contain the Holy Sacraments, the Body and Blood of Christ—until the Grail Knight finally undoes the damage and restores him and the land to health."

"Anyway, Allie," Charles says, shifting the subject, "I'm really looking forward to having a good look at those holy spears and lances. Maybe one of 'em's a close relative of the bleeding lance that Chretien describes in Perceval. Who knows, maybe in our presence they will bleed?"

"Fat chance of that, Charles Bascombe. As I recall, they only bleed in the presence of someone who is really, truly holy. Someone like Perceval or the Maimed King."

"You're suggesting we're not holy enough?"

"I wouldn't presume to speak for you, Charlie. But as for me, not a chance in hell."

❖

George Harpole, one of the men Charles had noticed on the Tor the previous day, sits alone in the Queen's Head pub, waiting for the waitress to bring him the ploughman's lunch he's ordered. George finds being alone a welcome change. He's in need of a break from Geoff Rawlinson, his friend and long-time colleague. Geoff has been riding him mercilessly the last two days, and George is sick of it. Not that he isn't entirely undeserving of Geoff's barbs. George has done what he's done, there's no getting around it. But was he *really* responsible for Nadja's death? Possibly he was, but he isn't entirely sure. In truth, he tells himself, she was the causer of her own death by simply having it in the first place and then by trying to hide it.

And really, George continues with his rationalizations, Geoff was as much to blame as he was—the whole thing had been Geoff's idea. "We can make a killing," Geoff had said, his words turning out to be unintentionally portentous. As for the so-called killing, they still didn't have the money; but, it shouldn't be long now. Anyway, George knows for certain that the object is safe and secure inside the hotel's safe. All they need to do now is complete the exchange and get the money transferred to the foreign account Geoff has set up. Then they'll be home free. Just as long as no one connects them to the dead girl.

That poor girl, George reflects. Why on earth had she turned up in Hull? She'd seemed to materialize out of nowhere, but what a godsend that had been. And how had she managed to come by the artifact? George has no idea. Had she unearthed it somehow in the museum where she'd been working, which George knew was in Eastern Europe—Krakow, or some such place? If so, had she stolen it? She must've known it was quite valuable. Damn good thing for him and Geoff she hadn't known just *how* valuable.

At last the waitress sets the ploughman's lunch down on George's table. He wastes no time cutting off a sliver of Double Gloucester and placing it atop a piece of bread he's broken from the square hunk on his plate. Then, drinking deeply from his pint of best bitter, he washes down the bread and cheese. Ah, just what he's needed.

The pub is crowded at the lunchtime hour, and now George looks about him to see if he recognizes anyone. Yes, several of them are fellow conference-goers. And then across the way he spots Professor William Wentworth, an acclaimed medievalist from Oxford, who is probably the most notable scholar in attendance at the conference. George doesn't know the man personally, but he's familiar with his work. The professor is having a ploughman's lunch as well, though his beverage appears to be cider rather than beer. George watches as the professor bites into a pickled onion, then wipes onion juice from his chin with a napkin. Professor Wentworth, George thinks, is precisely the sort of scholar he himself aspires to be—though he knows such that an aspiration will never be achieved.

❖

During the first of the afternoon sessions, Charles and Allie go their separate ways, Allie to one concerning Grail illustrations by the Pre-Raphaelites, and Charles to hear what Dr. M. Xander has to say about Islamic influences on the Grail Tradition. While they're doing that, the professor slips back to the hotel room for a nap. "Left Oxford at 6 this morning," he says. "I want to be daisy-fresh for the drinks party."

Allie's session is packed; she has to squeeze into a back corner and prop herself against a wall. Charles is one of only about a dozen people at Dr. Xander's talk, though they include several familiar faces. Eva Brooksby sits in the second row alongside the now-familiar cribbage players. A little farther back sits one of the fellows Charles had seen up on the Tor. He isn't with his friend and isn't wearing his flat cap, so it takes Charles a moment to recognize him. When he sneaks a peek at the man's name badge, Charles learns that the fellow's name is

George Harpole.

From the brief introduction of the speaker, Charles also learns that M. Xander's name isn't Mohammad after all, it's Mustafa. Charles finds the talk informative and provocative, and he likes the man's explanation for something Charles had long wondered about: the frequent occurrence of things in fours during the Grail Castle scene in Chretien's *Le Conte du Graal*: the four holy items in the Grail Procession (candelabra, lance, cup, and dish); the four-sided pillars and four-sided table in the castle's great hall; etc. In Islamic numerology, Dr. Zander points out, four is an especially important number. In contrast to Christian numerology where the number four only rarely occurs, for Muslims things in fours suggest the achievement of harmony and balance between the four elements of air, earth, fire, and water. The implication, Xander suggests, is that there is perfect harmony within the Grail Castle, home of the Maimed King and the Grail, harmony that contrasts with the chaos of the surrounding world.

At the second set of afternoon sessions, Charles, Allie, and Eva all sit together. Charles and Eva steel themselves for the predictable observations and clichés about the sexual implications of the lance and the cup they expect to hear from Mr. Martin Nicholson, Eva's Oxford acquaintance. Indeed, the man doesn't let them down, though most members of the audience seem to lap up his tired remarks.

"These ideas have been around for more than a century," Eva murmurs to Charles, who is seated between Eva and Allie. "Nothing here but titillating bullshit."

In the Q and A, someone asks the speaker about the oft-encountered phrase, "he was wounded through the thighs," and if that phrase is always a euphemism for emasculation.

"Often it is," the man replies, "though not always."

"Well, at least he got one thing right," Eva whispers.

❖

On that same Friday afternoon in a small town in Dorset, a slender, dark-haired schoolboy of twelve named Peter Saunders walks purposefully to the local bus station. His enquiries at the station are soon answered, and he's in luck. There is indeed a small local bus line whose route passes through Glastonbury and Wells on the way to and from Bath. Peter will need to catch the 8:30 bus, and the latest bus by which he can return stops in Glastonbury at 7 p.m.

It's perfect. He can be in Glastonbury before mid-morning and can have the whole rest of the day to explore its wonders. It will be his own personal quest for the Holy Grail.

Peter returns to his tiny room at the boarding school and begins assembling the few items he'll want to have with him—a light windbreaker; a collapsible umbrella; a small electric torch; the guidebook he already possesses; a pad of note paper so he can record his experiences; his camera, of course; and sunglasses and school cap, in case the British sun decides to behave more exuberantly than usual. He puts them all in his haversack.

Peter is so excited that night that he can hardly sleep.

CHAPTER 4
— Chalice Well —

After the final session, Charles and Allie spend a few quiet moments alone in their room at the Pilgrims' Inn. Then, at 5:30, they set off for the social gathering at Chalice Well. When they are still several hundred yards away from the entrance, they begin hearing sounds coming from the party.

"Sounds like we won't be the first ones to arrive," Allie says.

"Always chic to be a little bit late," Charles replies.

"Chic—just the word I would use to describe you, Charlie," she says with a laugh.

They produce their tickets at the entryway, and the man nods them in. They see a lovely expanse of garden before them, flowers and shrubs well-tended, walkways carefully laid out, and near the far back area, the surround to Chalice Well itself. Folks are spread about in little clusters throughout the garden, and quite a large group has congregated close to the Well. Two bars are positioned on opposite sides of the garden where the barkeepers are serving up a storm.

Charles and Allie pause for a moment just inside the entrance to take it all in. Charles notices that at the center of one of the larger clusters, folks have gathered about Mr. Bright-Rogers. They seem to be treating him like a rock star.

He's dressed in black tie, whereas most people in the garden are attired in what Charles thinks of as nice-casual. Some of the women, though, have donned fancy frocks, along with all the accouterments. He and Allie are dressed appropriately, he supposes, though just barely. Of Glastonbury's fabled New-Agers, there's nary a sign. They probably wouldn't have been granted entry, even if this gathering had been their cup of tea, which it surely isn't.

"Lead on," Charles says.

"No, you lead on," she replies.

"I'm the shy introvert here."

"Big fibber," she says. "You just trot out that line whenever you think it works to your advantage. Well, I suppose we should start off by imbibing the waters of Chalice Well, don't you think? Purify our souls, if such a thing is possible."

"Works for me," Charles says.

It turns out that for a pound a visitor can purchase a shiny-gold plastic souvenir chalice. Then, when their turn comes, they can help themselves to a cupful of the red-tinged water that gushes naturally from the well. People are lined up, eager to be able to say they've drunk from a chalice filled with the water of the holy well. Allie and Charles join the queue, and as they await their turn, Charles runs his eye about the garden. A lot of the people there have begun to look familiar, though he knows few of them by name. The cribbage players are there, and so is George Harpole with his usual companion, both of them wearing their flat caps. In another little cluster he spots Dr. Mustafa Xander who is chatting with a couple of the other speakers. Then he sees Professor Wentworth across the way in the midst of a small knot of scholarly-looking folks. That's Oxford contingent, Charles guesses, though he doesn't recognize any of them aside from the professor. Eva isn't among them, but then Charles does notice her. She's standing and chatting with another woman not far away from the Oxford group. This woman has the severe stereotypical look of the female Oxford don.

Charles hadn't really studied Eva closely before, but now he does. She's tall and thin with narrow shoulders; her elongated, oval face and pointed chin reminds him of a Modigliani model. Her dark eyes and face are framed by her scraggy brunette hair. Eva is certainly no beauty, Charles thinks a bit uncharitably, though she would probably appeal to men of certain tastes. As he's thinking those things, Eva glances up and sees Charles looking at her. She smiles and lifts a hand in greeting. Charles returns the gesture.

"Ah, it's your friend Eva," says Allie, who's just returned from a quick trip to the loo. "Nice gown, too. Once our chalices runneth over, we should go and say hello."

"I suppose we should," Charles says, without enthusiasm.

A few minutes later, as Charles and Allie are chatting with Eva, the professor, having slipped away from the group he'd been with, comes and joins them.

"Professor," Charles asks him, after they've all exchanged perfunctory greetings, "do you know a man named George Harpole?"

"Hmm, no, I don't think so, though the name does seem familiar. Ah, yes, I believe he's a medievalist at one of the northern universities, maybe Leeds or Durham? Why do you ask?"

"Everywhere I go, he keeps turning up."

"The two of you must have similar interests, Charles," Eva suggests.

"Yes, that's probably it," he replies.

"Well, Allie and Eva, since it appears that in a few months this likeable lad will be deserting us for the USA, why don't we drink a toast to him, eh? So here's to Charlie Bascombe, the pride of Waverly College."

"Hear, hear," says Eva. The other three take turns clicking their chalices against Charles', then they all gulp down some of their beverages of choice—wine or mead or ale—after having finished off their Chalice Well water.

"Ah," the professor says, "now that's what you call real ale. Aged in the wood, I believe. But, Charlie, before we start blathering about the talks you heard today, there's an important matter I need you to be aware of. You might even say it's a matter of life or death." The professor's words give Charles a sudden shiver, for he'd inadvertently overheard almost the same ones the night before.

"Sir, you have my full attention."

"Okay, then. Now listen carefully and don't forget. The chalice from the palace has the brew that is true. It's the vessel with the pestle that has the pellet with the poison."

Charles cocks his head, as if in thought. "Professor, let me see if I've got this straight. The chalice from the palace has the brew that is true. The pellet with the poison is in the vessel with the pestle."

"Quite right, Charlie, quite right. But unfortunately, there's just been a change of plan. Some klutz went and broke the chalice from the palace. They've replaced it by a flagon with a dragon. And now they've shifted the pellet with the poison from the vessel with the pestle and into the flagon with the dragon. So, don't forget, my lad. Now it's the vessel with the pestle that's the safe one, not the flagon with the dragon. Get it?"

"Got it."

"Good."

Eva shoots Allie a "what-the hell-is this" look. Allie just smiles. "When you've come to know these knuckleheads a little better, Eva, you'll realize that this sort of thing is merely par for the course."

"Gracious," Eva says. "So, professor, what you're saying is — the poison is now in the flagon with the dragon, *not* the vessel with the pestle?"

"That's correct, Eva. So long as there haven't been any more changes."

"But Sir, do you think it's safe for the spastic with the plastic," and she points a finger at herself, "to finish off her golden brew that's sweet as morning dew?" Without awaiting an answer, Eve lifts her chalice and downs what remains of her mead.

Her remarks cause them all to laugh.

"Eva, for shame," the professor says. "I don't need to remind you, do I, that we no longer use that word?"

"*You're* the spastic with the plastic?" Allie asks with an

impish smile. "That sounds a bit drastic."

Half an hour later they are startled by sudden shouts of "To the Tor!" And it isn't long before many others have joined in the shouting. In no time "To the Tor! To the Tor!" has become a mantra for the entire gathering.

Large numbers of folks begin moving toward the entranceway to the Chalice Well gardens, and soon a long stream of them file off to the left toward the foot of the Tor.

"Think we should join them?" Allie asks the others.

"Er," the professor says, "speaking just for me, I think I shall respectfully decline."

Eva is nowhere to be seen. Perhaps she's been one of the first to set off toward the Tor.

"What do you think, Charlie?" Allie says. "Even if we don't climb all the way up, maybe we could tag along and watch. Should be quite a sight."

And it is. Full darkness has now descended, and the long strung-out line of folks snaking its way up the steep path toward the top of the hill is clearly demarked by lights from their cellphones. For a moment Charles has a vision of Celtic tribesmen, centuries ago, climbing the Tor by torchlight. Now the sound of voices singing—singing loosely defined—comes floating down from the revelers on the Tor.

Charles and Allie, standing arm in arm, watch and listen for a few minutes.

"Charlie," Allie says, "it was a grand idea for us to come to this conference. The professor can scoff all he wants, but for me it's been nothing but a lark. The talks haven't been half-bad, really, and this strange mélange of people is fascinating. Best of all, though, I get to spend some time with you."

Charles smiles and gives her arm, interlinked with his, a squeeze.

Allie is right. Up until that point, at any rate, the conference has been pretty much a lark.

CHAPTER 5
— The Lance of Longinus —

Charles and Allie have just forty-five minutes in which to grab a light bite before the eight o'clock string quartet concert in the church. So they pop into the small vegetarian café on the High Street called The Good Earth. It's cafeteria-style dining, so they pause at the counter to consider a wide variety of salads, meatless pizzas, and quiche. When they've made their selections and paid, they carry their trays to one of the unoccupied tables.

Among the scattered diners are a few they now recognize from the convention, including Dr. Xander. He's sitting with an exotic-looking woman dressed in a flowing magenta gown with a matching silk head wrap. She's adorned with a dazzling array of baubles, bangles, and beads. "A woman like that," Allie whispers to Charles, "puts the rest of us frumps to shame."

"I'll take a frump like you over a woman like that any day of the week," Charles whispers.

"Is that your idea of a compliment, my dear sir?"

"She is quite stunning," Charles adds, "though not a patch on you."

Dr. Xander glances in their direction, and recognizing them, nods a greeting. Charles returns it by lifting his hand.

There's little conversation amongst the other diners, and Charles and Allie, being in a hurry, are happy to eat in relative silence also.

A light rain has begun to fall as they leave the restaurant, but since it's only a few steps to the church, they pay it little mind, and by the time they arrive, they are only slightly dampish. Church bells sound the 8 o'clock hour as they slip into a back-row pew.

For the next forty-five minutes they listen to short works by Scarlatti, Bach, Schubert, and Mendelssohn—a lovely, well-balanced program, Charles thinks. The audience is small but appreciative; the musicians—violins, viola, and cello—highly skilled; the acoustics in the spacious church excellent.

"All we need right now," Allie whispers, "is a visitation from the Holy Grail."

"Look there," Charles says, pointing up into the nave's high, dark, gothic vaulting. "See? There's the white dove descending slowly now; do you see the golden chain in its beak and the silver censer swinging gently beneath it? Oh, my. And now the fragrances of 'all the spicery of the world' have begun to fill the room."

"It's music that's filling the room, knucklehead," Allie says.

"Yes. Deliciously fragrant music."

There's no interval, and the program goes by quickly. When they've finished, the musicians take their bows to warm applause. As folks begin filing out, Charles and Allie remain seated in their pew and watch them pass by. M. Xander nods to them again as he and his female companion walk past. She smiles at them. Charles doesn't know the names of any of the others who were exiting, but several of their faces have become familiar to him.

As the church empties, Charles and Allie remain in their seats until they are alone in the nave. Then they stand up and begin making their way toward the north transept—where the replicas of the holy lances are on display in lighted cases. This, they think, should be an ideal time to view them without others being present.

The first three display cases, they find, are spaced out in the north transept, the last two in a small prayer chapel just off the transept. Allie stops in front of the first one, takes out her phone, and begins photographing. Charles edges up close and reads through the explanatory card on the inside of the glass-fronted case.

"This is a replica of the famous spear in St. Peter's Basilica," he says. "Looks to me like it might be a Roman *hasta*. My recollection is that Roman soldiers had two kinds of spears, the *pilum* for throwing and the *hasta* for thrusting. The Roman centurion who stabbed Christ in the side probably would have used the latter variety."

"A Roman centurion named Longinus."

"That's right—at least according to one of the apocryphal gospels."

"Charlie, look at the end of the spear? Doesn't it look like something's missing?" Allie says.

"Yes, the section that would have held the metal spear

point. Apparently, it disappeared a long while ago. No one knows how or why."

"Oh, wait a minute. I think I read recently that someone has actually found it."

"Someone *claims* to have found it," Charles says. "Just as a lot of folks over the years have *claimed* to have found the Holy Grail itself."

"Do I detect a note of skepticism from my learned friend?"

"What? I don't look like a true believer to you?"

"Hah."

They take their time studying the first three replicas, then move on into the small chapel to view the final pair. The fourth one is the one that was discovered in Antioch during the Crusades. To Charles it looks more like it might be a Saracen spear, although this is not an area in which he has much expertise.

"Oh, yes," he says facetiously, "that's the one that belonged to old Saladin himself. I remember it well. That one was his personal favorite."

"And you know that how? Because in a previous life you were right there with Saladin, the two of you fighting alongside General George Patton?"

"Actually, it wasn't General Patton, it was Richard Lionheart I was fighting alongside of," Charles says. "George decided to sit that one out."

"You and King Richard, fighting alongside each other. You must've cut dashing figures. Too bad you don't get to have a statue outside the Houses of Parliament like Richard." She smiles at him and says, "Of the two of you, I've always found you to be handsomer. And I'm certainly glad you don't share Richard's sexual predilections."

The last case they examine contains a true outlier. The huge lance is a brute of a thing. It's a good bit longer and thicker than the others, with a fearsome-looking barbed metal head. Compared to them, Charles thinks, it's like Babe Ruth's 36-inch, 42-ounce bat of American ash standing next to Barry Bonds' slender 34-inch, 32-ounce bat of Canadian maple.

"My word!" says Allie.

"Looks more like the kind of lance that would've been used for jousting in the High Middle Ages," Charles says. "It seems highly unlikely that a weapon of this kind would've been around at the time of the Crucifixion. That would be about twelve centuries too early. What I can imagine, though, is a medieval horseman being pierced through the thighs by a monster like this—a dolorous stroke indeed."

"What a gruesome thought, Charlie."

"Yeah. And even more gruesome if being stabbed through the thighs is a euphemism for being stabbed in another choice place."

"I've had my fill of these holy lances," Allie says. "It's going to be bad dreams for me tonight."

"What say we vamoose?"

"Si, amigo. What say we do?"

As they walk up the north aisle of the nave, Charles and Allie became aware of loud, angry voices coming from the vestibule. One of them Charles recognizes as the plumy, much-agitated, voice of Mr. Nigel Bright-Rogers. A second voice has the slight Scottish burr of Sorley MacPherson, the art historian from the Manchester Museum. Charles gives Allie's sleeve a little tug, and when she glances back at him, she sees him mouth the word, "Wait." They stop and stand where they are, a spot where they aren't in the line of sight of the men in the vestibule.

"This is neither the time nor the place to be having this discussion," Bright-Rogers insists. "Of course, we must have this discussion, but not here, not now."

"As far as I'm concerned," says a third voice, which Charles doesn't immediately recognize, "I want no part of any of this business. For me there's nothing to discuss. I don't care how much money is involved, you can count me out."

"Oh no," replies Bright-Rogers, "you are most definitely in, the both of you. We've gone too far and there is much too much at stake for anyone to be backing out now. Tomorrow during the lunch in the grounds of the Abbey we'll slip off to a secluded corner in the orchard and get this sorted, eh?"

"Well, all right then," says the voice of MacPherson. "For now, best sleep on this. That's what I suggest."

"Good advice," adds the third voice.

Charles and Allie listen as the footsteps move away. They wait until it's completely silent in the vestibule before exiting the church.

"Sounds like there could be nefarious goings-on tonight in old Glastonbury town," Charles says, as they walk back to the hotel.

"It's none of our affair," Allie says. "We should keep our

noses out of it." Then a moment later she says, "And yet . . . Charlie, did you recognize the voice of the third man?"

"The third man? Film with Orson Welles and Joseph Cotten?"

"Knucklehead."

"Oh, you mean *our* third man. Well, maybe. It sounded a little like the guy who gave the talk on the sexual implications of the lance and the cup. You know, Eva's acquaintance from Oxford, Mr. Martin Nicholson."

"You might be right. Speaking of Eva, I wonder where she's disappeared to?"

"Don't know, don't care," Charles says, with uncharacteristic force.

"Well, maybe she got lucky," Allie says.

"Hah!" Charles says. "Fat chance of that."

❖

George Harpole sits alone in the hotel bar's snug nursing a glass of single malt whiskey. As he waits for Geoff to turn up, his mind keeps returning to the events of that fateful night a month ago when Nadja, the attractive young woman he'd met several days earlier at the museum in Hull, had invited him up to her flat for a drink. When was the last time *that* had happened?

To George, the young, eastern-European woman was a real stunner. Probably in her mid-twenties, Nadja's face was framed by her lustrous, dark brown hair. She had deep-set eyes that were almost black, full lips, and a small round chin. Her body was slender and lithesome. To George she looked like he imagined Anne Frank might have looked had she reached early womanhood. George, a cautious chap at the best of times, planned to let Nadja take the lead in whatever might transpire. He would not try to play the role of seducer. For that, he was woefully out of practice, if indeed, he had ever been in practice. But if that was where things were headed, he would be a willing participant.

Nadja talked cheerfully about her job at the museum, where she was some sort of assistant curator. When he'd asked her about her previous life in Poland, she seemed reluctant to say much, though she did say she'd had a position in Krakow at the Wawe Castle. That was about it, aside from the fact that her grandfather had once been a friend of Oskar Schindler.

They'd talked of art and literature generally, and eventually the conversation had slid off in the direction of her work at the museum and to the subject of ancient artifacts. George didn't remember which one of them was responsible for that—at that point he was three drinks in—but somehow the topic of the Holy Grail had arisen and then, after a bit, the Spear of Destiny. She said she'd seen one of the alleged holy lances in a museum in Austria; George said he'd seen the one in the Vatican. "That's the one with the missing tip?" she asked. George said that it was.

No seduction occurred. That was kind of a relief to George, who knew he was frightfully awkward when it came to such things. But as he was taking his leave at the door, she'd placed her hands on both sides of his face and planted a very sweet kiss on his lips. "This has been nice. Can we do it again soon?" she asked softly. George nodded. "I would like that very much," he said.

He'd only seen her twice more—the final time was on a night that was far more momentous, far more fateful, than the first one had been.

CHAPTER 6
— A Game of Cards —

Evangeline Brooksby is enjoying a solitary walk in the rain, something she often does on rainy evenings in Oxford. Although there aren't as many lovely places to walk in Glastonbury as there are in Oxford, she still finds it pleasurable. She had enjoyed the socializing at Chalice Well and found the spontaneous exuberance of the group that climbed the Tor exhilarating. Now, though, she wants a little solitude—but *not* back in her dreary little room in the B&B.

Eva walks for an hour along the wet, deserted streets of the small town until her growling stomach demands sustenance. Not many places are still open, so she will probably have to settle for pub grub—microwaved lasagna, or some such thing. Still, that will be okay. What she doesn't need is more alcohol. She smiles as she feels the rub of the plastic chalice she carries in the pocket of her raincoat.

❖

As Charles and Allie enter the hotel lounge at 9:30, it is far more crowded than it had been the night before. Seeing the two empty seats at the card table and no game in progress, Allie seizes the opportunity and approaches the pair of cribbage players, "You chaps wouldn't be interested in a four-handed game, by any chance?" she asks them.

The slender blue-eyed man seated on one side of the table looks at the even slenderer brown-eyed man on the other. "As for me, having someone to beat other than Edwin would make a welcome change."

"Listen to 'im, will ya?" says the man whose name apparently is Edwin. "Bert beats me twice or thrice out o' ten, if he's lucky. But I do agree that playin' someone else would make a refreshing change, my dear."

As Charles moves to a chair on the far side of the table, Allie says, "I'm Allie. My laconic companion here is Charlie."

Charles, proving he's not totally laconic, says, "So you're Bert and Ernie?"

"Ha, ha. I'm Albert, he's Edwin. We're nobody's Muppets."

"And nobody's fools," adds Edwin, giving Allie a wink.

"I hope you fellows aren't sticklers for the finer points of the rules," Charles says. "It's been a while since my last cribbage game. If I miscount my hand, you won't go claiming all my points, I hope."

"You won't be making so many points you could possibly miscount them," Edwin says with a smile.

"Them're fightin' words, podner," Allie says sternly.

"I like a little gal with spunk," Albert says.

"Who you callin' little?" Allie shoots back.

They cut for the deal and first crib, then plunge eagerly into the game, which all four of them take seriously. As they play there's little chitchat back and forth other than the counting of points and the usual griping about lousy cards or piss-poor cribs. It's nip and tuck until the end, the game coming to a conclusion when Edwin pegs six points and moves their peg just across the line. They win by a single point.

"That was luck!" Allie exclaims.

"No luck about it, my dear," Edwin fires back.

"Pure skill," Albert says, chiming in.

At 10:15 Eva finds herself before the entrance to the Pilgrims' Inn Hotel. She knows that many of the conference attendees are staying here; indeed, if she had been slightly more flush with cash, she would have done that also. She enters the hotel, then directs her steps toward the residents' lounge; the sounds from the room seem warm and inviting. No one pays her any notice as she passes through the door. She stands just inside for a moment to size up the situation. A noisy group is watching a Premier League football game on TV. In an alcove near a window there's a card game in progress; two of the players, Eva realizes with surprise, are Charles Bascombe and Alwyn Tremayne. Two or three other small knots of folks are scattered about the room engaged in their conversations. Eva takes all of this in, feeling almost like a disembodied observer.

For a few minutes she watches the card game. They are playing a game she doesn't know but she can tell they are playing quite seriously. There isn't a great deal of joshing back and forth, though all four players seem to be enjoying the tense struggle. Charles' seat is beneath the window and faces the room. Allie sits across from him, her back to the room. Eva can only see the back of Allie's head of short, blondish hair, and her square, trim shoulders. She can't help envying Allie's looks. Some women, damn them, have all the luck.

"Excuse me," a man says from just behind her, "but would you allow me to buy you a drink?"

Startled, Eva swings about and looks into the round, bespectacled face of a man she's noticed at some of the conference sessions.

"How kind," she says. But then she raises her arm and steals a quick look at her watch. "Oh, dear, I am so sorry. I'm already late for meeting up with my friend. Do you mind if I beg off?"

"Maybe tomorrow night?" the man says hopefully. "I'm Dennis, by the way. Dennis Adams."

"Yes, well, perhaps tomorrow night then, Dennis." To Dennis's consternation, she swings herself about and scurries through the lounge door with the sudden movement of a startled rabbit.

Eva feels guilty at having been so rude, but she was caught completely off guard by the man's unexpected invitation. As she hurries into the hotel lobby, she runs smack into the more familiar figure of Professor William Wentworth. "Eva, just the person I was hoping to see. Why don't we step into the hotel saloon bar, eh? You'll surely let me buy you a drink."

"Yes, I will indeed. But only if you'll allow me to reciprocate." For Eva, the professor is a far less discomfiting presence than the unknown Dennis. Though now that she has her wits about her, she rather wishes she'd given the fellow a chance. Maybe, if there really was another invitation tomorrow night, she would give him that chance.

"Anything interesting going on in there, Eva?"

"Nothing much. Just some football game on the telly, for those benighted souls who are so inclined; and a few others who are engaged in some rather peculiar card game."

"I guess all the true intellectuals have found somewhere else to hole up. Or maybe they're all in the saloon bar. Let's go and see, shall we?"

❖

"Well played, you two," Albert declares, gathering the cards into a neat pile. "Not so rusty as you let on," he says to Charles. "I think you were sandbagging us. Would you fancy a rematch?"

"Not tonight, but maybe tomorrow. For now," Charles says, "could we just sit for a few moments and visit? Get to know you a little better?"

"I'll refresh our beverages," Allie says, getting to her feet. "Back in two shakes of a lamb's tail."

Charles and the two men sit without speaking until the silence begins to feel awkward. "Excuse my curiosity," Charles says, to get the conversational ball rolling, "but I saw both of you today at some of the Grail conference sessions. Are you fellas, by any chance, scholars?"

"Nope," says Edwin.

"Oh no," says Albert.

"What's the nature of your interest?" asks Allie, who's just returned with the tray of drinks.

"Just general," Albert says.

"Always wondered about that old Holy Grail," Edwin says.

"Wanted to see if I could learn a thing or two about it."

"We're retired widowers, you know," Albert says, "so we're free to go and do things such as this. We're the male counterparts to that bevy of blue-rinse ladies at the conference."

"You saw us there today," Edwin said, "and we saw you there today with Professor Wentworth."

"You know the professor?" Allie asks.

"*Everyone* knows the professor," Edwin declares.

"They do?" Charles says. "Everyone?'

"Man's a national treasure," Albert says. "Why, I've even seen him on the telly."

"I believe you know Dr. Xander, too. How is it you know him?" Charles asks with surprising directness. "He's not a national treasure, is he?"

"Dr. Xander? Don't think I know who you mean," Edwin says, clearly feigning an ignorance Charles doesn't buy.

"Oh," says Albert, "he means that Muslim chap who gave the talk. No, can't say we really know him. But I did quite enjoy his talk today. Most interesting. One smart fella."

"I missed it, alas," Allie says. "Went to a different session. Hard to be in two places at once."

"Yes," Edwin says with a smile, "that's a trick I've never quite mastered. Well," he says, "I think I shall be calling it a night. Getting late-ish for me."

"I won't be but a moment behind you," Albert says, "soon's I finish off what's left of this pint."

"And we won't be far behind you," Allie says.

When Edwin is gone, Charles asks Albert if they would see

him at any of the sessions tomorrow morning.

"If the creeks don't rise," he replied. "But you never know—there's quite a lot of bloody rain in this chilly little island of ours."

"I've noticed that," Charles says, "but to tell you the truth, it's one of the things I'll miss when I'm gone."

"And how soon will that be?" Albert asks.

"End of the summer. That's when it'll be time for me to go back home and earn my living."

"Ah, you academic chaps. You have a very good gig, as they say."

"Or as our mutual friend Professor Wentworth might say, 'Nice work if you can get it . . .'"

"'. . . and you can get, it if you try,'" Albert says, completing Ira Gershwin's lyrics. "Any idea where the professor is tonight?" he asks.

"Probably two hours adrift on a sea of sleep," Allie suggests.

After Albert has departed, Allie and Charles sit quietly and exchange puzzled looks.

"Now that's what I call a pair of tight-lipped blokes," Allie says. "They don't give much away, do they?"

"And you say *I'm* laconic. Allie, did you get the feeling they're not quite what they wish to appear?"

"I feel certain of it."

"Then what do you make of them? Police?"

"Possibly," Allie replies, "though I doubt it. Not ordinary plods, anyway. They're too subtle and sly. Maybe they're undercover somethings or other. I think there's a good chance they are."

"Something exotic like MI5 or 6?" Charles suggests.

"No . . . probably not those. But some government agency, I'd imagine."

"I wonder what the heck they're up to," Charles says. "Think they could be keeping a watchful eye out for nefarious doings in old Glastonbury town?"

"Hey, they're retired and free to do things like attending this Grail conference if they feel like it," she says. "And they seem to feel like it. Or so they say."

"Yeah, right. I'm sure Muslim Influences on the Grail legends are just what they've been *dying* to learn about."

Charles and Allie's card-playing friends are indeed two fellows worth speculating about, and their speculations hadn't been wildly off the mark.

Upon a cursory examination, Albert and Edwin look like two peas in a pod: slender men of middle height with thinning grayish hair, both in their late sixties, and both semi-retired widowers, as they had told Charles and Allie at the card table. But, in fact, they come from quite different backgrounds. Albert, an only child, is the product of an upper-class upbringing and was educated at a very good British public school—not Eton or Charterhouse, admittedly, but one of the second rank. Edwin's background is working-class—his father was a plumber, and he and his four siblings had been educated at a comprehensive in a Midlands industrial town.

Both men had ended up at Cambridge University, Edwin

by virtue of a scholarship, and both had taken PPE degrees (Politics, Philosophy & Economics). It was at Cambridge where they'd met and where they'd been recruited to work for a specialized division within Special Branch; and for the next forty years, that's where they'd been. Now retired, they are asked occasionally to take on some relatively minor task for the agency, something they enjoy doing. Physically fit and mentally sharp, they enjoy each other's company and enjoy a challenge. They are happy to assume the burden of some of the agency's lesser tasks when it frees up the front-line fellows for larger, more pressing responsibilities. The agency considers them a pair of old pros, and that's how they view themselves. Which is how they came to find themselves in Glastonbury at an academic conference on, of all things, the Holy Grail.

❖

Professor William Wentworth isn't two hours adrift on the sea of sleep, as Allie had supposed. He's about fifty feet away and very much awake. And to his surprise, he's rather enjoying Evangeline Brooksby's company. And she his, apparently. Eva had been feeling lonely, but she hadn't been bold enough, or maybe desperate enough, to cope tonight with the advances of the unknown Dennis Adams. But the more familiar and fatherly presence of Professor Wentworth she finds comforting.

Not far from them in the hotel bar sits George Harpole and his colleague, Geoff Rawlinson, the pair of flat-capped men Charles had first seen on the Tor. For the last few hours, these medieval scholars from Hull University have been ensconced in the snug of the hotel saloon bar. Like the professor, they'd eschewed the impromptu climb of the Tor as well as the string quartet concert in the church. Instead, they chose to sooth their troubled thoughts with drink. In George Harpole's case, he's been soothing his troubled conscience as well.

"You know I never meant for her to get hurt, Geoff," George says. "She was the one who came on to me. I would never have pursued her otherwise, much as I would have wanted to." He takes another sip of whisky.

Geoff just stares at him. Then he says, "Your turn is coming, George. You realize that, don't you? There's no avoiding it now, not even if we were to give it back. And we certainly aren't going to do anything drastic like that. Not with the kind of money that's staring us in the face."

"Stop them, Geoff. You must!"

"Not possible. Things have gone too far."

"But what can we do?"

"*We?*"

"I, then."

Geoff, his lips firmly compressed, just shakes his head.

"Look, there's the professor now," George says. "You know him. Introduce me to him. I'll throw myself on his mercy."

"George, that man is not involved. He knows nothing of any of this. He knows some of the players, but that's about it. Besides, I don't think there's much love lost between him and Nigel Bright-Rogers."

"Who's the woman with him?"

"Probably one of his Oxford protégés."

"Hmm."

"Leave them alone, George. Don't go getting yourself any deeper in the soup than you already are."

After Geoff has departed for his room, George Harpole remains there alone, He's in a funk. His whisky no longer holds any interest.

A little before midnight, seriously inebriated, George Harpole begins to ascend the hotel's dark staircase when he suddenly realizes that someone is standing motionless on the landing above him. A frisson of fear shoots through him. Then a familiar female voice says, "Hello, George."

George Harpole is too frightened even to scream. Finally, he manages to stammer, "But . . . but . . . Nadja, you're . . . *dead*."

"Yes, George," the female voice replies, "I am."

CHAPTER 7
— Glastonbury Abbey —

In the morning, Charles and the professor meet in the breakfast area for a quick bite while Allie enjoys a long and lazy sleep-in. The two men plan to attend a session on Lancelot's role in Malory's section on the Grail. While they're doing that, Allie plans to poke about in Glastonbury's funky little shops and boutiques. Then, at 10:30 they'll all three rendezvous at the Abbey for the special tour that's been arranged for conference attendees. After the tour they'll join all the others for a picnic lunch on the Abbey grounds.

"Which of the two weather reports did we get today?" Charles asks his mentor, "'Sunny with rainy intervals'; or 'rainy with sunny intervals'?"

"You know, Charlie," the professor says, ignoring his young friend's sage meteorological observations, "Chaucer didn't have a whole lot of use for the Arthurian legends."

"Apparently not," Charles replies. "I can only think of a couple of passing references to Arthurian characters in a couple of the tales." For William Wentworth, as Charles well knows, no other English author during the Middle Ages can hold a candle to Geoffrey Chaucer. And that includes Sir Thomas

Malory and even the vaunted "Pearl Poet," the anonymous author of *Sir Gawain & the Green Knight.*

"Well," the professor says, "'The Wife of Bath's Tale' is *ostensibly* Arthurian; but it isn't *very* Arthurian." He sets down his empty cup, then refills it halfway.

"Yes," Charles says. "And his comments on Lancelot—I can think of only two—are borderline snide. Speaking of Chaucer, sir, Eva recognized my name as that of the author of our little monograph."

"Yes, she mentioned that to me last night. Charlie, I believe the young woman is rather taken with you."

"Oh, lordy. In America, women hardly notice me."

"And here you have to beat 'em off with a stick."

"Well, hardly that. I think it's more likely to be a reflection on the so-called men who populate Oxford than anything else."

"Ha, ha. You might be right about that, Charlie. Perhaps you should stay in Oxford permanently. You'd enjoy quite an advantage."

"No disrespect, sir, but . . . no thanks."

"Can't say I blame you, my lad," the professor says seriously, "No, not one bit. And I have to confess that I envy your relationship with Allie." Way back in the Sixties, the professor himself had enjoyed a most stimulating year of graduate studies in the U.S. at UC Berkeley. That formative year had exerted a profound influence on his life and his values. And it had also initiated his life-long love of American music, American music of all varieties, not just the San Francisco groups of the late '60s.

❖

At the 9 o'clock session, the three Arthurian scholars on the panel offer brief observations about different aspects of Lancelot's role in Malory's Grail section. It's a lively session, and in Charles' view, the speakers' insights are quite worthwhile. In the Q and A, audience members ask a variety of questions, several that strike Charles as painfully inane, though the speakers manage to respond respectfully. Professor Wentworth does some eye-rolling but manages to curb his tongue, only emitting only a grunt or a low groan from time to time. Eva, at one point, elbows the professor in the side.

The cribbage players are in attendance as are the flat-cap chaps. One of them—not George Harpole, the other one— offers one of the better audience comments, which concerns Lancelot's possible apotheosis. "Do you think in the scene describing Lancelot's death that the Grail actually came for him and then accompanied his soul to heaven?" the man asks.

"That does seem to be what Malory is implying," the speaker replies, "though of course he doesn't make it explicit."

"Good answer," Eva whispers to Charles.

Listening to this discussion, George Harpole finds himself wondering about his own immortal soul. One thing he is certain of—the Holy Grail will *not* be coming to accompany his soul to heaven. Not after what he's done . . . or failed to do.

❖

During the bus ride to Glastonbury, Peter Saunders studies his map of the small town and decides that the first thing he should do is hike up Wearyall Hill. That site isn't far from where the bus will let him off. He remembers the American's questions about the hill from two days earlier. This brief exchange between the American and Peter's teacher has stuck in his mind. He's looked up Joseph of Arimathea, and he's encountered the intriguing conjecture that Christ himself—as a youth just a little older than Peter—might have come to Glastonbury in the company of his kinsman Joseph. When Peter read the lines from a poem by William Blake, it stirred him more than any poem ever had:

> *"And did those feet in ancient time,*
> *Walk upon England's mountains green*
> *And was the holy Lamb of God,*
> *On England's pleasant pastures seen!"*

Peter's bus arrives at the little station in Glastonbury right on time. It's just 9:30, and the hustle and bustle of a busy Saturday morning hasn't yet begun.

It's only a couple of short blocks to the street that leads up Wearyall Hill. As he walks along, Peter finds himself humming a tune beneath his breath. After a moment he realizes that it's a hymn they often sing at chapel services at school: "England's Green and Pleasant Land."

❖

Because so many people turn up for the tour of the Abbey, they decide to divide them into two groups leaving ten minutes apart. Allie, Charles, and the professor are in the second one, and Charles notices that the flat-cap chaps, as well as Dr. Xander and his female companion, departed with the first group. Albert and Edwin, the cribbage players, arrive just in time to join the second group.

"Missed you at the talk this morning," the professor says to Allie. "Couldn't resist the allure of all those wondrous boutiques, hmm?"

"All part of the Glastonbury experience," she replies.

"Any new tattoos in places you don't wish to mention?"

"That, sir, is my secret, and so it shall remain. By the way, these days it's called 'body art,' not tattoos."

"Body art," the professor scoffs. "Graffiti by any other name . . . ."

"The professor's body is his temple," Charles says. "No graffiti on the walls of *his* temple, Bubba."

"Too right," the professor agrees.

"Sorry to disappoint you, sir," Allie says, 'but as for tats, I'm as pristine now as I was before."

"What about Enya CDs?" he asks. "You buy any of those? Maybe some aromatherapy candles, a few healing crystals, some magic mushrooms? Pre-torn jeans? Surely you could find some of them."

"Ha, ha," Charles laughs. "I can just see Allie listening to Enya CDs on the drive back to Cornwall."

"Morning, all," sings out the cheery voice of Eva Brooksby. "Can I join you?"

"You may, if you can," the professor responds pedantically.

"Sorry, sir. Always getting my mays mixed up with my cans."

They haven't proceeded far into the grounds before the tour guide says, "And there, of course, is the holy thorn. Flowers twice a year. I'm sure learned folks such as you know all the legends about it. We hope we'll be able to get a cutting to grow up on the hill," and she points in the direction of Wearyall Hill.

She leads the group across to the Lady Chapel, one of the few buildings whose external walls remain intact. "This is the oldest structure in the Abbey. Although legend places the origins of this site in the sixth century, this is a 12th-century structure. It's Norman, or if you prefer, Romanesque. The north doorway you are now looking at must have been truly magnificent. Even in its present tattered condition, it's still quite lovely." There are murmurs of agreement.

"I believe that St. Gildas was said to have been buried inside this building," Charles says, causing the guide to raise her eyebrows.

"Quite right, sir," she agrees. "We don't usually point that out, since St. Gildas is no longer a household word."

"He was a fellow who had some very good innings," the professor remarks.

"Anyway," she says, wanting to get back to her scripted remarks, "it's the area just south of the Mary Chapel that's of particular importance."

"Where the bodies of King Arthur and his queen were first discovered," says Albert the cribbage player. He holds up his guidebook sheepishly to account for his knowledge.

"Ah, a well-informed fellow. Yes, sixteen feet deep in the earth. Presumably in an effort to thwart the vengeful Saxons, who feared and hated King Arthur for his victories over them. Later, the monks moved the remains of the king and queen to their final resting place inside the great gothic church at a spot we will visit in a few moments."

The tour continues—next up, the Abbot's kitchen; then the soaring but terribly battered walls of the Gothic church; and finally, the burial site marked for King Arthur.

"Now I'll lead you out through the orchard to where the picnic will be held. Any last questions before I do that?"

"Let's eat," someone says.

"Let's show our guide our appreciation," Allie says. Everyone in the group claps and cheers appropriately.

❖

Young Peter spends the better part of an hour atop Wearyall Hill. There is little to see, other than the sorrowful sight of the mutilated Holy Thorn and the glorious sight of the Tor a mile or two away. But it's a restful, peaceful spot, and after he photographs the remains of the Thorn and takes several shots of the Tor, the boy finds it a perfect place for undisturbed contemplation. No one else is around, which allows Peter to sit quietly and soak up the beauties of England's green and pleasant land without distraction.

A little before eleven, Peter ends his solitary meditations on Wearyall Hill and walks down to the Abbey. The area in front of the entrance is jam-packed with tour groups, so he spends a few minutes in the gift shop and waits for the tour groups to go on their way. As the final group is setting off, Peter spots the American who'd asked his teacher about Wearyall Hill, the man who'd told him about St. Bridget. The fellow had impressed him. Peter hopes he will get another chance to speak with him. He would like that.

After he sees the Abbey, Peter intends to visit Chalice Well. He's undecided about whether he will climb the Tor again, though he would like to and definitely will if time permits. Outside the Abbey gift shop he sees a notice about the Holy Lances that are on display in St. John's Church. That intrigues him. Maybe he can fit in a visit to see them. In fact, maybe he can write a school paper about them. The idea excites him.

But Peter remains conscious of the fact that the last bus back to Dorset departs at seven in the evening. He really can't afford to miss that bus.

As Peter wanders about the Abbey, it makes him sad to see how battered and bashed almost all of its structures are—before the Dissolution of the Monasteries, they must really have been something. Drat that Thomas Cromwell! What a dastardly fellow he'd been.

At least there is one structure that's still fully intact, the Abbot's Kitchen. Standing inside this remarkable and well-preserved octagonal building gives Peter a sense of what it must've been like to actually be there. Peter is in awe of the four huge fireplaces positioned in the four corners of the structure and of the louvered roof that allowed the smoke to escape. The small building has been fitted out with all the furnishings and paraphernalia of a real medieval kitchen. Peter tries to picture himself there, assisting the cooks in preparing a lavish meal. Perhaps, if he had lived then, he would have been one of the lads tending the cooking fires or basting a huge bird roasting on a spit.

For the better part of half an hour, Peter sits on a stool in a corner of the little building and allows his imagination to roam. Would he have enjoyed living in the fifteenth century? Yes, he decides, he most definitely would have.

❖

As Allie, Eva, Charles, and Professor Wentworth move out among the apple trees and approach the picnic area, the professor mutters, "How do you one-up the holy shrine to Thomas Beckett at Canterbury Cathedral?"

"Maybe you just happen to discover the body of someone even more revered buried in the grounds at Glastonbury Abbey?" Eva says, more a statement than a question.

"Indeed, a most fortuitous discovery. Pilgrimage was a lucrative business in the 12th century."

"As it still is today," Eva says. "Ever been to Lourdes or Santiago de Campostella?"

"Been to 'em both. How do you think my body has become the temple that it is?"

"You walked all that way to Santiago?"

"Just the last ten miles," the professor says. Took a public conveyance known as a bus for the first four hundred and ninety."

Ahead of them, standing with their heads close together, are Nigel Bright-Rogers, Sorely MacPherson, and Eva's Oxford don with the roving hands, Martin Nicholson.

"Professor," Charles remarks in a low voice, "I see your favorite person over there. Charles motions with his head in the direction of Bright-Rogers. The professor suddenly begins to intone a soft verse,

> *" 'I do not like thee Dr. Fell,*
> *The reason why I cannot tell,*
> *But this I know and know full well,*
> *I do not like thee, Dr. Fell.'*

"Actually, I do know the reason," the professor says. "In a word, the man's a prat."

As they watch, they see Dr. Xander approach the three men and engage them in a short but apparently heated conversation.

"The Antioch Lance," Dr. Xander says to the men without preamble, "I have to say that I am quite surprised you received permission to make a replica of it. I wouldn't have thought they'd allow that. I trust that you went through all the proper channels in order to receive it."

"We received special funding in order to arrange it," MacPherson replies. "All entirely above board, I assure you."

"Special funding? Sounds rather like bribe money to me," Xander replies harshly.

"Let's just call it an inducement, shall we?" Bright-Rogers says, smiling smugly.

"I'm sorry that you resorted to such an expedient. That lance is an artifact to be revered, it is not some crass commercial item. For many of us, it is a very sacred object. Its sanctity should have been respected. Copies of it should have never been permitted."

"Dr. Xander," Bright-Rogers says, "I assure you, the original object has always been treated with the utmost respect. And even though the replica is just a mere replica, it too will be treated with respect."

"I do not share the hostile attitude of some of my Muslim brothers to the Infidel," Dr. Xander says, "but when it comes to violating what should remain inviolate, I can understand their feelings—and, indeed, their actions." He turns away and walks over to where his beautiful companion has been standing and watching, a troubled look on her face.

As Allie, Charles, Eva, and the professor stand in the queue of folks waiting to fill their plates, a young female staffer from the abbey walks briskly up to them.

"Excuse me," she says looking at Charles, "but I'm seeking Mr. Bascombe, Mr. Charles Bascombe. Would you be he?"

"Yes, I am."

She holds out a slip of paper to Charles. "Your wife wants you to call her immediately in America."

"My *wife*? In *America*?"

For a moment no one says anything. It's Allie who breaks the silence. "I've always suspected that you were a bit of a dark horse, Charlie."

"Must be some sort of malicious joke," the professor says. "Charlie has no wife in America. When it comes to moral propriety, Charlie is straight as a Roman road."

Eva and Allie stand there waiting for Charles to say something.

"Well," he says at last, "I guess I'd better go call my wife in America. Anyone have a phone I could borrow?"

CHAPTER 8

— In The Apple Orchard —

Charles, holding Eva's phone, walks off into the trees to be alone.

For ten minutes his friends remain in the food line in silence, occasionally exchanging anxious glances. Finally they reach the long table where the food is laid out. Most of the other picnickers have already filled their plates and found places to sit.

"Umm, Scotch egg," the professor says. "Oh, yes, I believe I shall."

"Well, here comes our Charlie," Eva says.

"He looks rather relieved," Allie says, hoping her eyes don't deceive her.

"Guess what?" Charles says. "It was all a misunderstanding. It wasn't my wife who called, it was my boss."

"Wife, boss, often amounts to the same thing," mutters the professor to himself.

"The person who took the call," Charles continues, "thought the female-caller was joking when she said she was my boss. She assumed the caller was my wife. It really *was* my boss— she's the current Chair of the English Department."

"Damn," Eva says, "no American wife. How disappointing."

"What was so urgent?" Allie asks.

"They're putting the final touches on the class schedule for next fall semester. Wanted to be sure I would be coming back to teach my classes."

"Why wouldn't you be?" Eva says. "You thinking of sticking around in these parts? Hey, if you decide not to go back, maybe I could go over and cover the classes for you. How's that for a plan?"

"They'd heard a rumor," Charles continues, "that some other schools were trying to lure me away."

"Aha," the professor said, "our infamous Chaucer monograph. That thing has turned you into a highly sought-after commodity, eh, Charlie? Well, doesn't surprise me in the least."

"I am not a commodity," Charles says.

"Only an expression, lad, just a manner of speaking."

"Have you had any such inquiries?" Allie asks.

"Not that I'm aware of."

"Maybe if you opened your mail once in a while you'd know," Allie says. "You think that might be a good idea?"

"What? And spoil Mrs. Hawkins' fun? She gets a charge out of opening all my letters from America. I couldn't do that to her."

"Charlie," Allie says, "she's been on holiday in the Channel Islands for the last two weeks. You mean you haven't opened your mail during all that time?"

"You actually let someone else open your mail?" Eva asks, incredulous.

"I hope you don't let her open your email," Allie says, a slight blush suffusing her cheeks.

"*That* I don't do," Charles says.

"So, you assured your wife—I mean your boss—that you would be there in the fall?" asks the professor. "Wife, boss; boss, wife," the professor mumbles beneath his breath.

"Of course I did," Charles says. "Sir, I have no desire to be changing universities anytime soon."

The four of them seat themselves on a low retaining wall surrounding the monks' fishpond, balancing their plates on their laps. Half a mile behind them, the very top of Glastonbury Tor and St. Michael's Tower provides a picturesque backdrop. After a few minutes, Allie sets her plate aside and takes a photo of the others with her cell phone, getting the Tor in the background.

"Here, let me take one of the three of you," Eva says. "Oh, this will be a nice one," she declares. "Allie, you must send me a copy."

Not far away sit a group of older women who are chattering so loudly it's impossible not to overhear their conversation.

"That was a most fascinating session on Ley Lines this morning, wasn't it?" one of them remarks, receiving murmurs of assent. "I'd no idea so many of them converged on Glastonbury! Surpassed only by Stonehenge, the man said. The possibility that Joseph of Arimathea was drawn to Glastonbury by a powerful beam of psychic energy, why, that's simply amazing. You know, I think I can feel the energy from the Ley Line surging through me right now as we sit here. Can't you?"

"Margery," another woman said primly, "I believe the correct pronunciation is 'lee' lines, not 'lay' lines."

"The word 'lay'," another woman remarks, "often refers to something else." Her risque witticism causes a few titters.

"They're called lee lines," a third woman said, "because they pass through so many places with names ending in 'lee'— Bromley, Woodley, Greenlee, and the like."

"Professor?" Eva says quite loudly, "what's *your* take on Ley Lines?" Eva has asked the question only because she feels sure what the professor's response is likely to be.

"Ley Lines? Oh, Eva, Ley Lines are total shite. Only mental defectives believe in such things. If you think you'll find the Holy Grail at the end of a Ley Line—ha!— what you're likely to find is nothing but a big bag of . . . well . . . dog-dirt."

The ladies can't help overhearing the professor's comments, and a sudden hush comes upon them. Then, eventually a solitary voice says, "Well, I never!"

"Eva," Allie says sotto voce, "you are a bad woman."

Eva giggles.

"Professor," Charles says, "you're getting a bit irascible in your old age."

"I am, Charlie, I am. And I wish I weren't. But Charlie, all this nonsense these folks have been spouting about the Holy Grail, well, tends to put my teeth on edge, you know."

❖

Edwin and Albert—cribbage players and probably more than cribbage players—are seated on folding chairs not far from Charles and Allie's group. The two men are closely attending to the scene about them, with particularly keen interest in particular picnickers.

They watch as the trio of Nigel Bright-Rogers, Sorley MacPherson, and their Oxford don companion move off among the trees, apparently intending to have a private confab. They notice that Dr. Xander and his companion are chatting with a couple of the scholars who'd attended his lecture on the Islamic influences on the Grail legends. They're also keeping an eye on the pair of flat-capped chaps, just now returning from the food table with second helpings.

"Ah," Albert says, when he's spotted the little group sitting on the low retaining wall, "there's our card-playing friends, along with the famous professor and another young woman."

"I do quite like that spunky young woman we played cards with," Albert says, "I have to admit it. Wish she were wearing a dress rather than jeans, though. Guess I'll just have to imagine how nice her pins would look trouser-less. I'm not complaining, mind you."

"At our age, we'd best take 'em anyway we can get 'em, even with their jeans on," Edwin says.

"Oh, yes," Bert replies, grinning.

Nearer to them they overhear a man saying, "You do realize that Malory's work treats all the important topics found in all the greatest literary works."

"*All?*" another man says.

"Yes, all. Though of course in the great works there are really only two important topics—sex and death."

"Well, Malory's got plenty of both of those," another person

says.

"Do you think that fellow's correct?" Edwin asks Albert, "that there's just *two* important topics in all the great literary works?"

"Oh, yes, that's pretty much correct," Albert replies. "There's just the two of 'em—as long as you don't count the occasional whale."

As they're having this conversation, Albert and Edwin are unaware of the fact that sex and death have already loomed large in their current investigation—with more to come.

Dennis Adams, the bespectacled young man who'd spoken to Eva in the hotel lounge the night before, has been watching for another chance to speak with her. And when she gets up and goes to re-fill her mug of cider, he deftly intercepts her next to the table. "Oh, well hello again," he says brightly.

"Ah, if it isn't Dennis," Eva replies with a nod of recognition. "Hello to you, too."

"Do you think you might be able to spare me a couple of minutes?" Dennis asks her, hopefully. "It's really quite important."

"Sure. What's up, Dennis?"

"I have some questions I was hoping you might be able to help me with, questions concerning Oxford. Also, I was wondering about the man who gave the talk yesterday on the lance and the cup. You know him, I believe, and of course you know Oxford. As I say, it's quite important."

"Well, okay. Yes, I am slightly acquainted with the man,

although it wouldn't be accurate to say I know him well. And yes, Oxford is a place I'm very familiar with."

"Splendid. There's a couple of things I need to find out rather urgently."

"I'm game to try and help," Eva replies. "Could we walk while we talk?"

As the two of them, carrying their drinks, wander off into the trees to the east of the fishpond, several pairs of eyes focus on them.

"Eva seems to have picked up an admirer," Allie remarks to her companions.

"Or vice versa," Charles says. "Lucky fella," he says, with a grin.

"Oh, now, Charlie," the professor says. "You needn't be too hard on her. The girl can't help it if she tends to be a bit gauche sometimes. She's an Oxford bluestocking, for goodness sakes."

"Sir," Allie says sternly, "that is definitely a sexist remark. And, such a remark is definitely beneath you." But then after a moment's pause, she adds, "It is nice, though, that Eva's attracted an admirer."

"Allie! You sound like such a thing surprises you," the professor remarks. "That sounds a bit sexist to me."

"Eva is an odd duck," Charles says, "but not a total loser. She has some good points."

"A gentleman to the rescue," Allie remarks sardonically.

"She does have some good points, Charlie, she truly does," the professor says, hoping to mollify Allie.

"For one, she really knows her Malory," Charles says.

The professor frowns, then says grumpily, "Well, that's *something*, I suppose."

"Allie," Charles says, "have you realized that this brilliant Oxford professor standing next to us actually has some literary blind spots?"

"Yes, I have realized that, Charlie."

"Hah," the professor replies. "Ganging up on me, are you?"

CHAPTER 9

— Conversations in the Orchard —

Do you know who that chap is?" Edwin asks. He and Albert, one drinking coffee, one tea, have also been observing Dennis and Eva as the two of them move off alone among the trees.

"I do, actually," Albert says, as he sets his coffee cup carefully on the grass beside his chair. "He's called Dennis Adams. At least, that's the name he's used to register for the conference."

"And the young woman, what's she called?"

"Evangeline Brooksby. Prefers Eva."

"Ha, ha," Edwin laughs, "Adams and Eva. Well, they have plenty of apple trees to surround themselves with, even if those trees are months away from having any apples on 'em. No apples may be a good thing, by the look of those two. So, Bert, what's your reading of Dennis Adams? Think he could be one of ours?"

"Oh yes, I would say so. Probably Crumpets and Eclairs."

"Ah, a C & E man," Edwin says, referring to Customs and Excise.

"That's what I'm thinking," Albert replies. "One of ours but not one of *us*. Same genus, different species, so to speak."

"Think our concerns might coincide?"

"Don't know," Albert replies. "But whatever it is he's looking into, his cover seems a bit thin to me. Thinner than ours, at any rate."

"Do you reckon his interest in that young woman is just a part of his cover?"

"Oh no. I'd say his interest in her is quite genuine."

"There's no accounting for taste, is there," Edwin says.

"Oh, now, you're just partial to our young friend Allie."

"I am, I am, I readily admit it. That American lad, Charles, is a most fortunate fellow."

"Oh, to be thirty again," Albert says. He picks up his coffee cup and drains it.

❖

"They want us to wrap things up as soon as we can," Mr. Nigel Bright-Rogers says to his two companions, Sorley MacPherson and Martin Nicholson. "This weekend, if possible. And look, my friends, this is a lot of money we're talking about here. If we fork over the quarter of a million—and maybe we can bring that down a bit if we negotiate—we'll still be coming out way ahead. I mean *way* ahead. Our profits will sustain the museum for a good long while—and they won't do any damage to our own pocketbooks, either."

"But two hundred and fifty thousand pounds?" Martin Nicholson, the Oxford don, queries nervously, shaking his head.

"A quarter of a million to make five million?" Bright-Rogers replies. "What's not to like about that?"

"Not a bad exchange," says MacPherson, "even for a penny-pinching Scotsman like me."

"I should say so," Bright-Rogers agrees, smiling.

"But we still don't have the artifact," bleats Nicholson. "So how do we get it?"

"Aye, there's the rub," says the Scotsman.

"We shall have it tonight," Bright-Rogers declares, "one way or another."

"If it requires violence, I'm out," says the Oxford don.

"With the Spear of Longinus," Bright-Rogers says, "violence is always required." Seeing the horrified look on the face of the Oxford professor, he quickly adds, "That's a joke, of course. I'm tired of all the delays, too. So let's us get the bloody thing over and done with, eh?"

"Here's the note the hotel desk clerk handed me," Nicholson says. He pulls it from his pocket, opens the envelope, and studies it for a moment. "Ah, good. Yes, they say they want to complete the exchange tonight."

"Where and when, specifically?"

"In the prayer chapel behind the north transept—the smaller of the rooms where the lances are on display. At ten-thirty. We must be absolutely certain no one else is about."

"We give them the preliminary cash up front, and they hand over the artifact?"

"That's the arrangement."

"And we complete the wire transaction in the morning?"

"Precisely."

"When we have it," Sorley MacPherson asks, "then we let

the Vatican folks know?"

"Their representatives are in London at this very moment," Bright-Rogers says. 'They're prepared to take possession of it tomorrow."

"And our payday? How soon do we get it once we've handed the thing over?" Sorely asks.

"Just as soon as they've verified its authenticity. They say they should be able to do that within forty-eight hours."

"Are we 100 percent certain it's authentic?" Nicholson asks, nervously.

"I'd stake my life on it," Bright-Rogers replies.

"Let's hope it won't come to that," says MacPherson.

❖

Geoff Rawlinson and George Harpole sit well apart from the other picnickers. The two men are on pins and needles. Geoff because he believes he is about to become richer than he'd ever imagined possible, George because he knows they're skating on very thin ice. For him there could be major legal consequences, even if he manages somehow to get through this whole thing physically intact. The moral consequences of his actions he does his best to ignore, though his conscience is stressing. At the moment, though, his fear of death overrides his conscience.

"Things are set for us to make the exchange tonight," Geoff says.

"Good. How many of them know about it? The fewer the better."

"Just the three of them, and the two of us."

"What if they've concocted a plan we're not aware of? Maybe we should have a contingency plan of our own," George

says.

"That's not a bad idea. I'm not certain those blokes are completely trustworthy."

"What about this? I go over this afternoon and hide it in some little nook or cranny in the small chapel. We don't retrieve it from its hiding place until *after* they've forked over the initial cash payment and the signed contract. Then, if they try any funny business, we don't fork over the artifact. They'd be up a creek since we wouldn't have it on us and they wouldn't know where it is."

"Sounds like a simple but effective expedient," Geoff says. "Good thinking, George. Can you slide into the church and do it late this afternoon when no one else is present?"

"I can. I already have an idea of where to hide it, too."

Geoff smiles. He reaches out a hand and pats the shoulder of his friend. "My worries about your well-being, George, may have been misplaced. I felt sure those villains in Hull would be following us here. I've been keeping a weather eye out, and I have to say that I've seen no signs of them. Have you? George, it's possible that you'll survive this thing yet. Wouldn't that be something—alive, a free man, and a rich one to boot."

It would be something, George thinks, though he still has his doubts. He can't help remembering the strange hallucination he'd had on the hotel landing the night before. Thinking about it sends a shiver up his spine.

"You're dead," he'd said to the young woman.

"Yes," she'd replied, "I am."

❖

The second time George encountered Nadja had come a week after that first night when he'd had drinks with her at her flat. One afternoon after teaching his last tutorial of the day, on an impulse he popped into the museum hoping he might see her. There she was in plain sight, working at the information desk. When he approached, she looked up and gave him a dazzling smile.

After they exchanged a few pleasantries, she asked George if he would like to come and have another drink with her at her flat—tonight, if possible. He said he would, but only if he could take her to dinner beforehand. She hesitated, then agreed. She told him that she'd come across something very unusual that she was eager to show him, something she believed would interest him quite a lot. He asked her to bring it with her to dinner, but she declined, saying she would only show it to him in the privacy of her flat. She whetted his curiosity, no doubt about that. George decided he'd best be patient and find out what it was that she wanted him to see.

Dinner had been lovely. Although the city of Hull doesn't offer a great many first-class dining places, there are a few, and George booked a table at his favorite one. French cooking on the northern seacoast of England! At least Hull was a place where fresh seafood was plentiful, and the imported French chef was truly a marvel. They'd shared a bottle of Grand Cru Burgogne along with their shellfish medley.

Afterwards, they'd lingered over coffee. Then Nadja had said, "So, George, I actually have two treats for you. Both of them at my apartment." She gave him a look of invitation.

George Harpole was a dead duck.

❖

By mid-afternoon on Saturday, the streets of Glastonbury are teeming with shoppers, tourists, and the usual assortment of New-Agers. Charles, Allie, the professor, and Eva, who'd rejoined them after her tete-a-tete with Dennis, had remained in the Abbey grounds until most of the other picnickers had departed. As they push through the exit now, Charles notices their cribbage-playing friends walking ahead of them, probably heading back to the hotel to have a game.

"Charlie," the professor says, "Allie has already explored the shops, but what do you say you and I do a little of it, too. I should pick up some knickknack or other to take back to my wife."

"Charlie should pick up something for his American wife, too," Eva says. The look on Allie's face says she's not amused.

Suddenly they hear the sounds of chanting and the booming of a bass drum. The sounds are coming from the upper end of High Street and are growing louder. A group of bizarrely appareled men, women, and children come straggling down the street toward them—to Charles they look like a mélange of medieval peasants and Sixties hippies. As they get nearer, a rhythmic pattern of sounds emerges: "*Boom, boom, boom*— 'Have you found Jesus?'—*Boom, boom, boom.* 'Have you found Jesus?'"

Two of them carry a large banner with "HAVE YOU FOUND JESUS?" emblazoned across the front of it. Their rotund and gray-whiskered leader, who wears a battered top hat and an old baggy pair of corduroy trousers held up by a rope, carries a long walking stick which he waves before him. Charles thinks he looks a bit like a drum major leading a rather rag-tag marching band. A very bizarre drum major leading a very mal-synchronized bunch of marching idiots.

"Jack Straw or Wat Tyler would have nothing on that old geezer," the professor says, referring to two notorious figures from the late 14th-century.

"It does look a little like the Peasants' Revolt come to life, doesn't it," Charles remarks.

As the motley assortment of men, women, and children draw nearer, a wild-haired woman reaches out and grips Eva by her forearm. She declares ecstatically, "I've found Jesus, I've found Jesus!"

"Oh, well done," Eva replies with a straight face. "And where was he?"

In the next moment the crowd has flowed on down the sidewalk, some of them crowding out into the street, forcing people to step aside and cars to creep by cautiously.

"That woman could have been the model for Bruegel's Mad Meg," the professor says, with a shake of his head.

"Mad bunch of nutters," Eva says. "Well, that's Glastonbury for you."

❖

Two men—the very ones Geoff Rawlinson has been worrying about—sit in a pub just across the street from the entrance to the Pilgrims' Inn Hotel. At mid-afternoon on Saturday, the Lamb & Plough isn't busy, and the men have seated themselves near a window that looks out onto High Street. The street teems with people and activity, but what the men care about are the people going in and out of the hotel.

These are not prepossessing-looking men. One is tall and thin, his ferret-like face featuring a long and sharply pointed nose. His small, close-set eyes are as black as coals. His burlier companion has almost no neck, but a wide and nearly lipless mouth, and black, bushy eyebrows. Inside the pub they are hatless, but they still wear their jackets—with the collars turned up.

Their attention on the hotel entrance is interrupted for a few moments by the appearance of the religious zealots who come marching down the street chanting to the accompaniment of their bass drum. "Strange folks," the thin one mutters. His companion gives a silent nod of agreement.

The men return to their surveiling, and after ten more minutes they suddenly come alert. They watch Dennis Adams cross the street and enter the hotel.

"Interestin' chap, that one," mutters the thick-set man. "Looks like he could be p'lice."

"Like as not," replies the other. "Might hafta deal with 'im, but we can't be killin' no p'liceman."

"If we hafta, I can deal with 'im without doin' for 'im." The burly fellow pats the side pocket of his jacket.

"Let's wait on that, eh? Later tonight, if it becomes necessary."

"All you hafta do is you say the word." The men's words indicate their familiarity with lower-class British slang, though their pronunciations betray their Central-European origins.

As they continue watching, they see quite a few people they assume are conference attendees enter the hotel, including Professor Wentworth, Charles, and Allie. But none of them thus far are the people who hold the greatest interest to them.

Then they see a couple of folks who do, the two professors from Hull.

"That be them," says Ferret-face.

"Aye. And we best get our hands on 'em 'fore they try to move it."

"Which I think they're likely to try and do tonight. They'll want to do the transaction in some dark and private place. More'n likely, in the church."

"I'm thinkin' you're probably right. Still, don't like it that there be p'lice about. Someone else, somehow, seems to've got wind o' what's a-goin' on."

"It does looks like it," says Ferret-face. "But we'll manage it."

"Aye, that we will." The burly man pats his jacket pocket again.

CHAPTER 10
— In the Prayer Chapel —

As Peter approaches the church door he sees the sign: "Church Closed until Sunday Morning Services." He's disappointed that he'll have to miss out on seeing the holy lances, but at least that will give him plenty of time to make one more visit to the Tor. Still, the boy can't help himself from reaching out and trying to turn the great iron ring that operates the door latch. It turns. Peter pushes against the heavy door, and when it opens a crack, he slips through and shuts it quickly after him. Surely, he thinks, no one can object to his going in and taking a quick peek at the lances. There can't be any harm in that. He won't touch a thing, just have himself a good look.

Peter passes through the vestibule quietly, then, entering the nave, he stands still for a moment listening. As far as he can tell, he's totally alone in the dim and cavernous church.

Enough late-afternoon light shines down through the high windows in the nave for Peter to find his way easily to the north transept. A large window in the north wall of the transept provides sufficient light for him to locate the cases containing the holy lances. Each of the cases, he discovers, has a light switch. But to be on the safe side he chooses not to turn them on. Instead, he uses his small flashlight to read the information on the cards.

Peter takes his time inspecting the different lances. He stands before each case jotting down bits of information on his note pad. He's already familiar with the biblical story of the soldier who pierced Christ's side, but he's never heard of the *Gospel of Nicodemus* or that there was a Roman centurion named Longinus. Peter finds the objects themselves extremely fascinating.

The last two display cases are in a separate prayer chapel just off the North transept. This small, windowless room lies in semi-darkness, so Peter needs to use his flashlight to locate the cases. He spends a few minutes examining the first of the two lances, then turns his attention to the final one. Compared to the others, this huge spear has quite a different appearance; Peter finds this one especially intriguing. Just as he is jotting down some notes about this last spear, his keen ears pick up the sound of footfalls coming from the direction of the nave. Someone else has come into the building. Now the steps are approaching. Since he isn't supposed to be in the church, his instincts tell him it would be better if he weren't found here.

Peter glances about in search of a hiding place. There seem to be few obvious possibilities. Then he spots the narrow space between the case he's been looking at and the wall behind it. Maybe he can squeeze himself into it. With his foot Peter nudges his haversack into a small opening beneath the display case, then he eels himself into the narrow space behind it. It's tight, but with an effort he manages it.

The footsteps he's been hearing cease for a moment outside

the prayer chapel. Then they begin again. Now someone enters the small, dark room where Peter is hidden. Peter holds his breath. Whoever it is, they've just flicked on a flashlight. Peter is pretty sure he won't be visible unless the person comes and shines his light directly into the small opening behind the display case. He hopes he's shoved his haversack back far enough to be out of view.

For a long moment there's nothing but silence. Peter feels chills of excitement and fear running through him. Then, to the boy's ears, it sounds like the person has stepped over to the wall opposite the case behind which he is hidden. The person seems to be doing something there. Peter can't see what that might be since his line of sight is blocked by the display case he's behind. After another moment, the sounds stop. Then Peter hears a man's voice say softly, "Well, that should do the trick." The man must've been speaking to himself. Now, Peter hopes, the fellow will leave.

But he seems in no hurry. And now, footsteps are advancing toward the case shielding Peter. Then they stop. Peter knows his discovery is imminent. He hopes he can squeeze himself out of his hiding place and make a dash for it.

He hears a man's laugh. "Who could ever imagine that a lance like this one was used at the Crucifixion? Absolute piffle."

For another minute, more silence. "Ah, Nadja," Peter hears the man say with a sigh. "We had a few wonderful hours. What a shame it couldn't continue. I am so, so sorry they did that to you."

It sounds like the man is moving away. It isn't until Peter

hears the steps retreating from the room that he dares breathe a huge sigh of relief. He doesn't know how long he's been crammed into his little hidey-hole. However long it has been, it's been far too long.

Peter remains where he is until he hears the man's footfalls diminishing as he moves through the nave. Eventually, they disappear altogether. Peter patiently waits for another full minute, then slithers out from behind the case. He gives his arms and shoulders a good stretch. Golly, the freedom of movement feels good.

Until that moment, Peter's mind has been wholly occupied by whether or not the man would discover him and what might happen if he did. He hadn't given any thought as to why the man had come or what he might have been doing in the room. Now he does.

Peter goes over to the display case on the other side of the little room to where he thinks the man has done whatever he's done. Slowly Peter's eyes, aided by his small flashlight, scan the entire area. He can see nothing different from when he'd looked at this case earlier. He shines his light on the wall stones and inspects them closely, but again he sees nothing unusual or amiss. Then he looks at the gap between the case and the wall. This gap is far narrower than the one he'd slid himself into on the other side of the room. In the wall, at about chest height, Peter notices a horizontal line of stones that extrude from the wall maybe an inch or two more than the others.

Peter directs the flashlight's beam into the gap and runs it along the wall. Has something been shoved in there at arm's length? Is something now perched on the stones? Holding the light in his right hand, Peter snakes his left arm into the small opening. His fingers brush up against something. The object is fairly narrow and Peter grasps it between his thumb and index finger.

Carefully he extracts his arm and looks at what he holds in his hand. When he shines his light on it, he can see that it's a small wooden box. It looks like a box that might contain a pen and pencil set or maybe a woman's necklace. Peter lifts the hinged lid. Inside, there's an object wrapped in cloth. Peter slowly unwraps the object and examines it closely.

What is it? It's certainly not any kind of jewelry; nor does it look like anything he's ever seen before. Most of it is just a simple, slender piece of smooth wood. At the end of it, fitted onto the piece of wood, there's a metal cap piece that ends in a sharp point. The metal is dull looking but not rusted. Peter hefts the object in his hand and contemplates it. Then it slowly dawns on him what it must be—it's the *head of a spear*.

What should he do with it? He certainly won't take it. Should he just put it back where he'd found it? Yes, that's what he probably should do. That's what his schoolboy code of ethics requires him to do. But as he thinks about it, he also realizes that his schoolboy code of ethics requires that the man who'd left this thing, a fellow who'd scared the tar out of him, should be suitably rewarded. That man deserves to have a good scare himself. It's not an act of vindictiveness, Peter tells himself. More like a harmless prank. The idea of it causes him to smile.

Peter knows that he must leave the object in the small prayer chapel where he's found it—he is no thief—but he decides that what he should do it is relocate it just a little bit. He won't leave it *precisely* where he found it in order to cause some confusion; but he'll leave it close by so that it can be discovered with just a little bit of effort. Peter wants the fellow to feel some of the same panic he caused Peter to feel. That would only be fair— wouldn't it?

So, where could he leave it? As Peter considers the possibilities, he sees that the display case in front of where the object has been stashed has a flat top with a slightly raised edge. Standing on tiptoes, Peter places the small box on it. The top of the box still shows a little above the raised edge, but it's unlikely to be noticed unless someone runs the beam of their flashlight directly over it. To Peter, his little ruse seems perfectly fair.

Peter wishes he could wait around and see the man's reaction when he can't find the little box. But he's used up far too much time already. He has a bus to catch. He hopes he can still make it. He knows he's cutting it close.

CHAPTER 11
— Friends When You Need Them —

With a sick stomach Peter watches as the little bus pulls away from the pickup point. It swings through the round-about half a block away and heads off en route to Peter's destination in Dorset—*without* Peter on it. If he'd been just two minutes earlier, he would have made it, no problem. Now what should he do?

The boy has little money, no place to stay, and knows no one in Glastonbury. On top of that, he hasn't eaten since lunch. Peter has always been an upbeat boy, confident in his own resourcefulness and resilience. At the moment, though, he feels bewildered and defeated. And now, wouldn't you know it, a light drizzle begins to fall.

Peter looks over at the high wall surrounding the abbey. Maybe he can discover a way to get in; then he could camp out overnight in the Abbot's Kitchen. It would be warm and dry in there, and maybe he could even scrounge up something in there to nibble on. That possibility helps to cheer him a tiny bit.

"Peter?" comes a man's voice. "Is that you?"

Peter looks up to see the young American scholar from

Oxford with whom he'd exchanged words on the Tor Thursday afternoon. With him is a woman Peter doesn't know.

"Are you okay?" the man asks. "You look a bit downcast."

"Sir, I've gone and royally messed up. I've missed the last bus to get me back to school. Now there's no way I can get there. Won't be another bus until tomorrow. And not many buses run on a Sunday."

"Peter, this is Allie. And I'm Charles."

"Hi Peter," she says.

"Hello, miss," the boy replies.

"Are you hungry, Peter? Allie and I are on our way to meet a friend at a Chinese restaurant. We'd be pleased to have you as our guest."

Peter is too shy to admit it, but right at this moment Chinese food sounds wonderful.

"I wouldn't wish to be a bother, sir," he says.

"A bother?" Allie says. "Peter, it would be our pleasure."

"While we eat," Charles says, "we can consider your predicament, see if we can't figure out what it might be best to do. How far is it back to your school?"

"Maybe forty miles. It's close to Dorchester, sir. Roughly an hour's drive."

"If we can't get you back there tonight, we'll get you there tomorrow."

"But sir, I have no place to stay tonight."

"There's a small sofa in our hotel room that probably wouldn't be too uncomfortable," Charles says.

"Or the professor may have an extra bed in his room," Allie

suggests. "We can ask him. Most of the hotel rooms are double-bedded, and I'm sure he wouldn't mind."

"Yes, that would be better yet," Charles agrees. "And it would give Peter a chance to become acquainted with one of Britain's most celebrated personages."

The boy looks at Charles as if he must be kidding. But he isn't sure. "Really?" the boy says.

"Oh, yes," Allie replies with a smile. "And I promise you that you'll find the professor a fascinating and most knowledgeable man."

Ten minutes later the four of them are seated together in the Golden Pagoda restaurant sipping tiny cups of hot Chinese tea.

"How about a spring roll, Peter?" the professor asks. "Would you like that? How about a couple of them to begin with?" The boy smiles and nods.

"Works for me, too," Charles says.

"And for me," Allie says.

"Sounds like spring rolls for four to start with," the professor tells the waitress. "We'll need a few minutes to decide on our entrees."

"Tell us about your day in Glastonbury, Peter," the professor says to the boy. "What did you do? What did you especially like?"

The boy is nervous, with the three adults all looking at him, waiting for his response. Slowly he summons up his courage and begins. "I really liked that view of the Tor from up on Wearyall Hill. It was splendid. After I first learned about Wearyall Hill from Mr. Bascombe on Thursday when our school group was here, I studied up on it. Read the verses from William Blake's poem and all the legends about Joseph of Arimathea and the Holy Thorn."

"I love that view too, Peter," Allie says, giving him a smile of approval. "You're right, it is truly splendid."

"And visiting the Abbey ruins was very cool," Peter continues. "What a terrible shame all those buildings were so bashed about; I'm glad that they spared the Abbot's Kitchen. I spent a long while in there watching the people in their old-time outfits, doing their chores with those ancient tools. That was fascinating."

"Charlie," the professor says, "I think we have an incipient medievalist on our hands."

"*Incipient?*" Peter asks, with a tilt of his head.

"Fledgling," Allie says.

"*Medievalist?*" Peter asks.

"One who studies the Middle Ages," the professor says.

"The Middle Ages? Oh, I guess you're talking about the Dark Ages."

"Probably better to refer to that thousand-year period as the Middle Ages, Peter," Charles says. "The so-called Dark Ages have had something of a bum rap. They weren't nearly so dark as people often assume."

Peter's face bears a look of perplexity. "Attila the Hun? The Black Death? The Inquisition? The murder of Thomas Beckett in Canterbury Cathedral?" Peter has obviously been studying for his school exams.

"Yes," the professor says, "all those things did happen. But over a span of many centuries, a lot of terrible things can occur. Look at all the truly awful things that happened in just one hundred years during the twentieth century."

"World wars, the Holocaust, the Atomic Bomb and the Cold War, all those horrible assassinations," Allie says.

"In my country," Charles adds, "we still had slavery until about a century and a half ago. But anyway, Peter, go on with telling us about what you enjoyed seeing today."

Peter tells them how he slipped into the church to see the replicas of the holy lances. But there is one detail he thinks it best to omit. When it comes to the small box he'd discovered and relocated, he decides to remain mum. He isn't sure they would approve of what he'd done. And in truth, he's been having a twinge of guilt about it himself.

As the meal progresses, the lad's initial anxieties of being with these unfamiliar adults dissipate and his natural exuberance resurfaces. The warm welcome of his new companions and the warm food in his belly helps to make him far less trepidatious about having missed the bus and being stranded in Glastonbury.

As they eat and talk, Peter looks over his new friends carefully. The old Oxford professor looks exactly the way he imagines an Oxford professor should look—his face a bit craggy and desiccated, his gray hair sparce and unruly, his clothing rumpled and untidy. The younger American professor, however, doesn't match Peter's idea of a scholar at all. When he'd first seen Charles Thursday afternoon up on top of the Tor, the man had reminded him a little of Gareth Bale, the famous Welsh footballer. Charles has the same lean and lanky athletic build, the same longish light-brown hair and blue eyes. As for Allie, Peter is totally in awe of her. The boy is at an age when he's just beginning to notice girls—an interest that's been delayed by the fact that he attends an all-boy boarding school—and Allie perfectly fulfills his idea of what an attractive young woman should be, with her lively personality, her trim but shapely figure, her short and wavy honey-blonde hair, not to mention having the rosy-cheeked face of an angel.

"Was there anything you saw today that you might wish to know more about?" the professor asks the boy.

"No, not really. I sort of understand why that Thomas Cromwell fellow did what he did to the Abbey—though it was a terrible shame that he did those things. What I really don't understand, though, is why someone had to go and whack down the Holy Thorn up on the hill."

"Whoever did that," Allie says fiercely, her hackles up, "should be skinned alive and roasted slowly over a bed of red-hot coals."

"And I'll bring the marshmallows," Charles adds.

The boy, startled by these comments, glances toward the professor.

"Don't look at me, Peter. You're the one who brought up the Inquisition."

Peter is silent for a moment, but then a smile appears on his face. Then he begins to laugh softly, and when he does, the others join in, their laughter not as subdued as his.

As the meal progresses, Peter feels more and more at home

with his trio of new friends. With them, he knows he will be all right. Maybe he will even learn a thing or two. In fact, he realizes, he already has.

After brushing his teeth with the spare toothbrush Allie had in her purse, Peter, wearing just his underclothes, crawls into the extra bed in the professor's hotel room. Charles is settled in an overstuffed chair reading his P.D. James novel.

"Want me to stay here till you've drifted off, Peter?" Charles asks him.

"Oh, no need to do that, sir. I'll be fine." The exhausted youth pulls up the duvet and in less than ten minutes he's fast asleep. Charles remains there reading for a few more minutes until he reaches the end of a chapter. Then he turns the light down to its lowest setting and slips quietly from the room.

While Charles is tending to Peter, the professor and Allie have retreated to Charles's room to wait for him.

"Any chance of us having a cup of coffee?" the professor asks. "It's become bloody hard these days to get a good, honest cup of coffee, what with all these blasted corporate chains trying to take over the world."

"Sounds like you're not a Starbucks fan."

"Hah. No, Allie, not so much."

"Charlie's fussy about his coffee, too," Allie said. "He actually brings a little stash of his own personal blend. I could brew you a cup of that right this minute, sir, if that appeals." The professor gives her a thumbs-up.

"Allie," the professor says as she's making the coffee, "I know it's none of my business, but I can't help wondering what the future holds for you and Charlie."

"I've been wondering about that myself," she replies.

"You mean you haven't talked about it?"

"A little but not a whole lot. When it comes to the future, Charlie tends to be even more laconic than usual. I know he's thought about it some, but he hasn't shared all of his thoughts with me yet."

"What about your thoughts?" the professor asks. "Have you shared them with him?"

"To be honest, I'm still sorting my own thoughts out."

"If you went with him," the professor says, "I'm sure you would like America. I did. And I'm certain America would like you. Why, goodness sakes, America even liked *me*."

"I've been wondering about all of that. Okay, Sir, coffee's up." She hands him a cup. "You prefer just a little bit of creamer, right?"

"You remembered. Allie, I hope you realize what a fortunate woman you are to have a talent that's completely portable. Unlike most couples, you and Charlie wouldn't have to worry about one or the other of you needing to compromise their career to accommodate the other."

"I guess that's true. But, I'm just not sure that I want to leave the U.K. Most of all, I hate the thought of leaving Cornwall. And, I'm afraid it would break daddy's heart if I did."

"Your father has a heart? I thought he only loved his old books. Just kidding, Allie. I know how important you are to him. Anyway, there's one good thing about an academic career like Charlie's. His summers are usually free, and he has a lot of long vacation breaks. The two of you could still spend a good bit of time in the U.K., and even Cornwall, if that's what you desire."

"I dearly love Charlie," she says. "But I'm not sure he's ready to cast his lot with me."

"Oh, dear, oh dear. Well, the lad could hardly do better," the professor says.

"And, to be perfectly honest, I'm not sure just yet if I want to cast my lot with him. I *think* I do, but . . ."

The professor looks at her with raised eyebrows and pursed lips. "Allie, that's a question only you can answer," he says, after a short pause. "But it's wise not to rush into a thing until you are completely sold on it."

❖

After having a lovely meal together at Glastonbury's only Greek restaurant, The Flying Horse, Eva Brooksby and Dennis Adams have taken themselves to the saloon bar of the Pilgrims' Inn Hotel where they are enjoying an after-dinner drink. Tonight, Eva is making an effort to look her best and be on her best behavior. Dennis finds her an enchanting companion. He's never dated an intellectual woman before, and for him Eva, with her puckish sense of humor and her wide-ranging mind, is definitely a different cup of tea. Captivated by the woman, Dennis has a hard time keeping his thoughts focused on the case he's been sent to Glastonbury to investigate.

When he feels his mobile phone vibrate in his pocket, his

mind quickly jumps back to business. He knows it's important that he take the call, so he asks Eva if she'll excuse him for a moment. "Sorry, just need to make a quick trip to the Gents. Back in two ticks," he tells her.

"Of course, of course," she replies.

After fifteen minutes Dennis hasn't returned. Eva begins to grow anxious. What can be keeping the fellow? After another fifteen minutes, growing more irked by the second, Eva concludes that Dennis has gotten cold feet and ditched her. He's not only ditched her, but the S.O.B. has also stuck her with the bar tab. Fortunately, she remembers Dennis's hotel room number and tells the girl to charge the drinks to his room.

Eva's highly favorable opinion of Dennis is undergoing a major revision. Drat it—he'd seemed so promising, too.

It isn't quite ten o'clock, and with no desire to return to her dreary room at the B&B, Eva decides to take another late-night stroll, as she so often does in Oxford.

A light drizzle—hardly more than a mist—is falling as she steps out of the hotel. She stands and thinks for a moment, then directs her steps toward a section of the small town she hasn't yet explored. As she walks, her disappointment begins to ebb slowly away. But damn that Dennis, she can't help saying to herself. He'd seemed so genuinely interested in her. He isn't too bad looking, either—in fact, she finds his owlish face and round glasses kind of cute—and he actually seems semi-intelligent. Cute and intelligent, a combination of qualities she hasn't often found in the men who've shown an interest in her.

Eva pulls a scarf from her coat pocket and ties it over her

head. With the collar of her coat turned up, she strolls off through the misty rain.

❖

In the hotel bar, George Harpole sits alone nursing a glass of Johnny Walker Red. Geoff had a couple of drinks there also but then deserted George and headed off to his room. Tonight, George thinks, I stand a chance of becoming a wealthy man—just as long as I don't become a *dead* one.

Poor Nadja. Was there any way he could have prevented her death? There are so many unanswered questions. Did Nadja know what the artifact truly was? If she did, then why had she been so anxious to hand it off to him? Was he merely a convenient mechanism for keeping it out of the hands of someone else? She'd certainly known the power she had over him, so maybe she'd assumed she could persuade him to return it to her, if need be. If she did assume that, George knew she would have been right.

Had the whole thing been a setup? Had he and Geoff been duped? He doesn't think so. Not if the artifact is what he believes it is.

But who was it that killed her? George has no idea. Maybe, he thinks, she'd managed to steal it from someone, and when they discovered what she'd done, they made her pay a heavy price. If he hadn't been so ready and willing to take it from her, maybe she could have been able to return it. Then, maybe she'd still be alive. George deeply regrets that he bears some responsibility for the young woman's horrible death.

He can't get that final, horrible image out of his head—the

image of this beautiful young woman lying on the floor like that, her arms extended on each side of her, the palms of her hands bloody, a huge gash in her side. Someone with a grisly sense of humor had made her pay a terrible price for giving George the artifact.

George is now on his fifth or sixth drink, but the truth is he's lost count. He's staring down into his glass when he senses the presence of someone on the seat at the bar next to him. He swivels his head to the right to have a look. His bleary-eyed vision tells him it's a woman. It's Nadja.

"Nadja?"

"Yes, George, it's me." It really is her, though George is having a hard time bringing her into focus. Too much whisky, he supposes.

"Nadja, where'd you come from? H-how'd you get here?"

"I came to warn you, George."

"W-w-warn me?"

"Yes, George. You must stay away from the church tonight. You mustn't go there. It will be bad."

"Things at the church will be b-bad?" George feels unsteady on his bar stool. He puts a hand down atop the bar for stability.

"Yes, George, they will." Nadja brushes back a stray lock of her dark hair in a gesture George has become familiar with, a gesture that endears her to him.

"How w-will they be bad? And how do you k-know that?"

"I just do. Trust me, George. Stay away. Can you do that?"

"Well, I guess I c-could get Geoff to go by himself. He won't like it."

"You must do that, George. Promise me."

George's eyes stray back to his nearly empty glass. The last half inch of whisky no longer holds any interest to him. When he raises his eyes to look at the woman, she's no longer there.

"Nadja?" he whispers. "Oh, Nadja, please don't go."

The barman has been keeping an eye on this man who's been sitting there alone mumbling to himself. He knows the fellow has already surpassed his limit. He won't serve him another drink.

The drunk man's lips are moving and the barman can just barely make out what the man is saying: "More th-things in h-h-heaven and earth, Hor-ra-tio, than found in your ph-ph-los-o-phy."

The barman has seen quite a few drunks in his time. Academic drunks, in his experience. are in a class of their own. He's often seen them sitting alone having a quiet conversation with Johnny Walker.

CHAPTER 12
— A Silent Night, An Unholy Night —

Tonight, Albert and Edwin are not playing cribbage in the residents' lounge. They've parked themselves in comfortable chairs inside the hotel's main lobby at a spot where they can keep a close eye on people's comings and goings in and out of the hotel.

At 8:45, they see Professor Wentworth, Allie, and Charles come in. With the threesome is a young lad of eleven or twelve. Where did he come from? The men exchange wondering looks.

At 9:00, they watch as Dr. Zander and his lovely companion enter the hotel and climb the central stairs. A few minutes later, it's Eva Brooksby and Dennis Adams who come in. They head toward the bar. Not long after that a man enters the hotel who they haven't seen before, a stocky, black-coated bloke with a sour look on his nearly lipless face. They haven't seen him at any of the conference sessions, and he doesn't look like an academic. Is he someone they should be concerned about?

About 10:15, they watch as Eva crosses the lobby and leaves the hotel. She leaves alone. Where's Dennis? A few minutes after that, the black-coated fellow also leaves the hotel, still with a scowl on his face.

It's now reached an hour when most folks have headed off to bed, and Edwin and Albert still haven't seen any of the particular folks whose comings and goings they're especially interested in. Finally, one of them does appear. It is nearly half past ten when Geoff Rawlinson, one of the professors from Hull, strides across the lobby and exits through the hotel door. Edwin nods toward Bert, who nods back. Then Bert heaves himself slowly from his chair and saunters after the man. Edwin remains in the hotel keeping watch alone.

Geoff hadn't wanted to be the one to complete the transaction with Bright-Rogers and his pals; he'd wanted George to do it. But George is so hammered by the time he'd come up to the room that it wouldn't be a good idea for him to even be there, let alone do the whole thing on his own. Geoff had been the one who'd set it all up, but he'd hoped he could keep a low profile and let George be their front man. After all, it was George who'd obtained the artifact from the woman he called Nadja, someone Geoff had never actually met. Geoff wasn't sure that George was in any physical danger, but he'd played up that angle to keep George in line. George could be a bit of a dense head sometimes, something Geoff had often used to his own advantage.

Geoff knows, though, that these are dangerous waters they've waded into. These days sentiment has turned against Britain's long-established habit of snatching up antiquarian treasures from other countries. Just look at all the hullabaloo about the Elgin Marbles in the British Museum and the outcry to return them to Greece. It remains to be seen where that will end up. But anyway, even though this is totally new territory for him, Geoff knows that there are government officials keeping a close eye on the antiquities trade, and that they'd better play this thing very close to the vest.

It was probably illegal for them just to have the artifact in their possession, even though they themselves hadn't done anything illegal to obtain it. In any case, the artifact would soon be out of their hands. And then, falling into their hands, should be a very big pile of cash.

When Albert leaves the hotel, he immediately crosses to the opposite side of the street and directs his steps in the same direction up the High Street as the Hull professor has gone. Albert watches the man swing left onto the walkway that leads to St. John's Church. Should he follow him, or should he wait for him to come back out? Albert chooses to do the latter. He spots the dark entranceway to a small shop across the High Street that will provide him with a convenient place from which to keep watch. There he'll be out of sight and also out of the light rain that's begun to fall. There's even a concrete ledge on which he can perch his bum while he waits. All he lacks is a flask of black coffee. Well, he thinks, you can't have everything, can you?

Geoff Rawlinson enters the dark church and makes his way to the north transept. As he enters, he sees that the space is dimly illuminated by a small battery-powered lantern. Two men are there awaiting him. Geoff doesn't recognize either of them—that's a bit of a surprise—but he hopes they have the money. One of the men is short and barrel-chested, the other leaner and sharp-faced, his sizeable nose the most prominent feature of his face.

"Just you?" Sharp Nose says to him.

"I don't know you," Geoff says. "Did Bright-Rogers send you? Are you working on his behalf?"

"Bright who? Don't know who you mean," the man replies. "We're not working on someone else's behalf. Just on our own."

"You did bring the money, didn't you?" Geoff queries nervously. It's dawning on him that something here doesn't seem quite right.

"Enough mucking about," the stouter man grumbles. "Where the hell's the bloody artifact?"

"I don't understand," Geoff says. "Are you rival buyers?"

"We're not *buyers*, wanker. It's our artifact. We want it back—*now*."

Geoff stands there speechless. What's going on? The deal is going down the drain fast. And these two chaps don't look like gentle playmates.

"Nadja, the fucking bitch, stole it from us," the sharp-faced fellow says. "She had no business passing it on to you. You just hand it over now, then you'll get through this all right. You start arsing about with us, you won't."

These men, Geoff realizes, speak with slight central or eastern European accents. And now that he thinks about it, he realizes that he *has* seen them before, though he can't recall where or when precisely. Maybe it was in Hull.

The shorter one slowly extracts an object from a side pocket of his jacket. It looks like it's a cosh. The other bloke moves up close to Geoff. He seizes his right arm and jerks it behind his back. He has Geoff in a painful hammerlock.

"Where *is* it? You got it on you?" He gestures with his head for his mate to come and search Geoff.

"No, no," Geoff says, "I don't have it on me. It's in the next room, safely tucked away."

"Then come and show us."

"Let go of my arm and I will."

The man lets go of Geoff's arm, but not before giving it a painful upward jerk. When Geoff lets out a yelp, the man chuckles.

The three of them move into the small prayer chapel behind the north transept. Frightened, Geoff struggles to recall where it was George told him he'd hidden the thing. Yes, now he remembers. George said he'd jammed it into an opening behind the left-hand display case.

"Find the feckin' thing," the stout one says. "Do that, there'll be no fuss, no muss."

The stout fellow carries the small battery-powered lantern and sets it on the floor. Geoff scans the room quickly, then steps toward the display case against the left wall. Yes, there's the narrow gap behind it, just as George had described. Geoff shines the light from his cell phone into gap. He doesn't see anything. He can just snake his slender arm into the narrow opening. His fingers touch nothing.

"Bring the light over here," he says to Stout-man. Looking

skeptical, the man does.

"Shit," Geoff says, "there's nothing in there. Maybe this is the wrong case, maybe it's behind the other one." But it isn't.

"Find it, wanker," Nose-man says.

"I'm *trying*," Geoff bleats.

"Try fucking harder," Stout-man says.

Finally, Geoff just shrugs his shoulders. "Don't know what to tell you," he says. "George was drunk. Must've told me the wrong damn thing."

"That don't let you off the hook, arsehole," says Big Nose.

"Listen, I'll go back to the hotel and check with him again, eh?"

"The hell you will. You'll go nowhere, wanker." The stout fellow is tapping the cosh in the palm of his hand.

"What the hell!" Geoff shrieks. The cosh suddenly smacks against his skull just behind his right ear. Geoff goes down like a felled tree.

The two men set to work on him immediately. Their intention is to send a very clear message: you arse around with us, this is what happens to you.

Neither of the men notices the small wooden box perched atop the left-hand display case; if one were attentive, he could see the top portion of the box just above the raised edge of the display case. It's too bad they haven't been more attentive. It's especially too bad for Geoff Rawlinson.

❖

Albert hears rapid footsteps. Two men suddenly appear and Albert jumps to full alert. They must've come from inside the church, he thinks. To him their movements seem highly suspicious, even furtive. One of the men, the stockier of the two, might be the same unknown fellow he and Edwin saw pass through the hotel lobby earlier. The slimmer man he doesn't recognize. With dismay he watches as they scurry up the High Street away from the center of town. Should he follow them? Then he thinks about the professor from Hull who'd gone into the church. What has happened to *that* bloke?

While Albert is dithering, three other men suddenly enter the picture. These are men he *does* recognize—they are Nigel Bright-Rogers, the Scotsman Sorely MacPherson, and their Oxford don compatriot, Martin Nicholson. This little group heads for the church also. Monitoring the activities of these chaps has been high on his and Edwin's list, so Albert decides he'd better remain at his post. As far as he knows, those other unknown chaps who are hotfooting it up the High Street may have had nothing to do with anything. But he isn't at all sure about that.

Bright-Rogers, MacPherson, and Nicholson disappear into the dark church. Albert considers following them but chooses to remain at his station. And then—less than two minutes later—the threesome suddenly reappears. They come rushing pell-mell out of the church, Nicholson in the lead. He seems to have gone into panic mode. He charges off heedlessly up the High Street like a runaway horse. His companions shout for him to stop, but he ignores them. Bright-Rogers and the Scotsman stand beside each other looking frightened and flustered. They exchange a few muted words, then they, too, head off in different directions, MacPherson moving down toward the hotel, Bright-Rogers striding across the High Street and then aiming himself toward the pub on the corner.

Albert watches from his dark alcove as the man passes by, just a few steps away; he waits a tiny bit longer, then follows after Bright-Rogers. He thinks he hears the man muttering, "What the hell? What the bloody hell?"

It's 11:00 when Edwin sees Professor Wentworth coming down the central staircase. The professor waits alone in the lobby a couple of minutes before he's joined by Allie and Charles. The threesome exchange a few quiet words, then turn and move toward the hotel door. Although this trio isn't among the people he and Albert suspect of possible misdeeds, Edwin can't help being curious about what they could be up to at this hour of the night. His instincts tell him he should follow them—so he does.

Edwin steps out in front of the hotel just in time to see Charles, Allie, and the professor as they swing left onto the walkway leading to the church.

CHAPTER 13

— Saturday Night & Sunday Morning —

Peter, exhausted from his many exertions of the long day, has fallen asleep in the professor's extra bed. He's deep into his dreams by the time Charles tiptoes quietly from the room. It is sometime later when a loud noise from outside the room jolts the boy from his slumbers. It takes a moment for him to get his bearings. Where is he? Not in his tiny room back at school. It finally comes to Peter that he's in a hotel room in Glastonbury, a hotel room that he's sharing with an eminent professor from Oxford.

But what was the loud noise that's awakened him? Wanting to know, Peter slips from beneath the bedcovers. He pulls his trousers on over the underclothes in which he'd been sleeping. Barefooted, he creeps to the door, opens it cautiously, and peers out into the dimness of the hotel hallway. Nothing—the corridor is quiet and empty. Peter isn't satisfied. He sets the door lock on the latch so he can get back into the room, then slips out into the hallway to investigate.

At the far end of the hallway near the landing, there's something lying on the carpet in a heap. Peter approaches cautiously. As he gets nearer, he sees what appears to be the dark form of a person sprawled out there. Peter creeps up close and peers down. It's a man lying on his back. He isn't moving. He utters no sounds. Peter notices the slight up and down motions of the man's chest and breathes a sigh of relief. As he looks the man over, he sees no wounds or blood. Has the fellow passed out? Has he had a heart attack? Is he inebriated?

Whatever the case, Peter knows he must find help. He steps over the body and hurries down the central staircase. The lobby is empty and no one is attending the reception desk. Spotting a call bell atop the desk, Peter punches it again and again. "Hello?" he shouts out. "Hello! This is an emergency!" Finally, he hears footsteps coming from a room in back of the reception desk.

"All right, all right, keep your shirt on, I'm coming. And who the heck are *you?*" the sleepy-eyed fellow snarls at Peter.

"There's a man lying on the floor of the hallway just beyond the landing. I think he needs a doctor. Right away." Peter glances at the wall clock behind the reception desk. It's 11:10.

Just then another man comes across the lobby.

"Can I help?" he asks. The man is Dr. M. Zander, though Peter doesn't know that.

"There's a person lying on the floor upstairs near the landing," Peter says. "I think he needs a doctor."

"I'm a doctor," Zander says. "Let's us go and have a look, shall we?" To the desk clerk he says, "To be on the safe side, would you please call for an ambulance."

"Are you sure, sir?"

"Just do it, okay? Now, come and show me, son. And what

is your name?"

"I'm Peter."

"Hello, Peter. I'm Dr. Zander."

"Are you from . . . London?" Peter asks, noticing that the man looks kind of like a Middle-Easterner.

"Yes. But not originally."

While Dr. Zander takes the man's pulse, Peter stoops down and retrieves the pair of round glasses he sees lying close to the body.

"He's got a strong pulse," Dr. Zander says. He's already noticed a contusion on the back of the man's head. "But that's quite a bump the fellow's had. He's likely concussed. If so, he'll need to be hospitalized. Peter, run down and see if the deskman can round up some ice. We'll ice his head until the EMTs arrive."

"On my way, sir," the lad says, and hops to it.

❖

Charles Bascombe and his two companions turn onto the walk leading to the church. As he glances up, Charles sees the outline of the church's imposing 15th-century tower traced against the dark sky. As he does, a line from a familiar poem shoots into his head.

"*'Is there anybody here, said the Traveler, knocking on the moon lit door,'*" Charles says, quoting a verse from the Walter de la Mare poem.

"*'Tell them I came, and no one answered,'*" Allie says, also reciting a line from the poem.

"*'That I kept my word,'*" the professor says, chipping in.

"What are the chances that somebody's tucked away inside the building listening to us?" Charles asks.

"A few lonely church mice, perhaps," the professor says.

A moment later they hear a familiar voice say—"Listeners? Do I count? Me and those lonely church mice?"

"Evangeline! Good gracious, young woman," the professor says, "what are you doing out here howling at midnight?"

"Not howling, just some innocent prowling. Surely you realize that I've nothing but a dreary little room in a B&B to return to. I've no warm and cozy hotel room like some folks do. And, sir, what's *your* reason for being out here howling at midnight?"

"A dreary little room. Ah, Eva, the joys of the academic life. You'd best get used to it. You probably have thirty more years of those joys to look forward to. Why are we out here at this hour? Thought we might slip into the church and take a peek at those blessed holy lances—I've yet to see them. Would you like to join us?"

"I haven't seen them either," she says, "so yes, I'll join you happily."

As they approach the door, they see the sign saying the church is closed; like several others before them, they don't hesitate to enter when they discover the door isn't locked.

The building lies mostly in darkness, but they can see well enough to pass safely through the vestibule. They stand for a moment at the back of the nave as their eyes adjust to the darkness of the vast interior, illuminated only by a few dimly lit sconces spaced out along the exterior walls.

"Lead the way, Charlie," the professor says in a whisper, not wanting to disturb the quietude of the empty sanctuary.

The four of them move over to the left-hand aisle and walk single file toward the north transept. When Charles passes the pew where he'd first met Eva two nights earlier, he smiles at the recollection of his initial encounter with this eccentric young woman who asked him if she could borrow his program.

They enter the north transept and Allie and Eva flick on their cell phone lights. The professor, who's brought a more powerful flashlight, turns that on as well. Charles is light-less but doesn't mind, since he's already taken a look at the lances. He's here mostly just to keep Allie and his old mentor company. The four of them spread out before the exhibitions and take their time studying them. "There are light switches on the cases," Charles tells them.

"Ah, so there are." The professor flicks on a light. "Let there be light," he says.

❖

Edwin is a minute or so behind Charles and his companions when he, too, enters the dark church. He works his way silently to the front of the nave, then stands there out of sight and listens to the voices he can just barely hear coming from the north transept.

"The missing spear head," he hears Charles say, "would it have been made of iron? Or maybe some metal alloy?"

"Iron, most likely," comes the professor's reply, "though from what I've read, there's a range of possibilities—including iron, bronze, and various kinds of stone, including flint."

"Why was Christ stabbed in the side?" Allie asks. "Just

another aspect of the gruesome torture and execution?"

"The side wound was Christ's fifth and final wound," the professor says. "But unlike the others, it wasn't part of the torture. Its purpose was to reveal whether or not Christ was still alive."

"When the water and blood gushed from Christ's side," Charles says, "it showed that He wasn't dead—dead bodies don't bleed."

"That was when some of His blood splashed down onto Longinus's face," Eva says. "It was Christ's holy blood that miraculously cured Longinus's blindness."

"Well, . . . ahem," the professor says, sounding grumpy. "That *is* one of the medieval legends. But Eva, there's no scriptural authority for that detail. It's not found in any of the gospels. Strictly apocryphal, my dear."

"Maybe it's not in the gospels," Eva replies, "but that's the tradition Malory draws upon when he has Galahad restore the sight of a blind man at the gate to the City of Sarras."

"You and your Malory," the professor scoffs.

"You and your Chaucer," she replies in an equally mocking tone.

"You two can just knock it off," Allie says. "Or Charlie and I will be tempted to use those holy lances on you—and see if we can get any blood from *you*."

"No point in that," Charles says. "Those two are bloodless, unfeeling zombies."

"Har," the professor snorts.

"There's two more cases in the prayer chapel," Allie says.

"Kinda dark in there, though."

"Well, let's us just go in and have a look, shall we?" Professor Wentworth says.

He follows Allie into the small room, Eva and Charles right behind him. He flashes his light at the left-hand case by which Allie is standing; and as the light moves across the case, Allie notices something perched on the top of it. The professor then swings his beam of light across the room to the display case against the other wall and holds it there for a few seconds. Finally, he brings it back toward the middle of the room. He directs the light beam down toward the floor in front of them. There it freezes.

The four of them stare down at the gruesome sight now fully illuminated by the professor's powerful beam of light. A man's body is lying there carefully arranged on the flagstones. His arms extend from his torso at 90-degree angles; his legs are stretched out straight and crossed at the ankles. His hands have been turned palms upward. At the center of his palms are small bloody puncture wounds; they look like stigmata. A single puncture wound is visible in his top ankle. His bottom ankle, which isn't visible, presumably has one also. On the right side of his chest his torn and blood-soaked dress shirt displays a large stab wound.

"Oh, sweet Lord Jesus!" Eva moans, "the man's been *crucified.*"

"Yes, after a fashion," the professor replies, "though at the moment he's sans cross, spikes, and crown of thorns. I wonder if there were spikes and if so, what's happened to them. Strange, that. Did he, she, or they take them away? Why would they? The spear I think we can account for," he says, glancing over at the glass-fronted display case against the right-hand wall, whose door is not fully secured. "That's a case that displays a bleeding lance!"

"Does anyone know who this poor chap might be?" Eva asks.

After just a brief pause Charles says, "Yes, I believe I do."

Then they hear a man's loud voice coming from behind them. "Everyone! Please, just stand still right where you are. And please, don't anyone touch anything. Now if you would, could you all just start backing slowly out of the room."

They see that the man behind them is holding up some official-looking credential in a leather folder. Allie recognizes him. He's one of the cribbage players, the one named Edwin.

"Don't touch anything," Edwin has said to them—but for Allie, his command has come a little too late. For when the professor first flashed his beam of light into the room and ran it across the left-hand display case, she'd noticed something poking up atop the case. Instinctively, she'd reached up and grabbed ahold of it. Right then it was too dark for her to get a good look at it, so she'd stuffed it into her shoulder bag to look at later. Now she's embarrassed by what's she's done.

Oh, well, she thinks, it's probably not anything of any importance. I can tell the man about it later. Right now he's got more important things to worry about.

CHAPTER 14

— The Morning After The Night Before —

Neither Charles nor Allie is eager to think about the events of the previous night—or to be more precise, *the* event of the previous night—the gruesome sight of that body which had been so carefully arranged on the chapel floor. Neither of them has fully processed what they'd seen during that brief moment before Edwin shooed them out of the prayer chapel. Charles finds himself wondering if what seemed to have happened really had happened. But no, he knows it did. What the four of them had seen was very real. But he hasn't any notion what it was all about.

Charles recognized the man lying on the floor. It was Geoff Rawlinson, a medievalist from Hull. Charles first saw the man atop Glastonbury Tor on Thursday afternoon in the company of his colleague, George Harpole. Someone did something truly awful to poor Geoff Rawlinson. But *why*? Charles has no idea. And where was Harpole? Could he have had something to do with this? Again, Charles has no idea.

Fortunately, Charles and Allie have Peter to help take their minds off of it. Peter, lucky and plucky lad, knows nothing of that event, though they discover he had an adventure of his own.

Now as the three of them are seated in Allie's car, on their way to Peter's school in Dorset, the boy regales them with his discovery of an unconscious man lying in the hotel hallway. It's obvious, as he chatters away, that he's in awe of Dr. Xander, the man who'd joined him in assisting the injured man. Charles, too, has been intrigued by Dr. Xander, ever since one of the ladies checking off names in the church foyer had mentioned him. And then even more so, after he heard the man's inspired talk about the Islamic influences on the Grail legends.

Last night's drizzle is long gone, and it's an absolutely beautiful Sunday morning in April, a perfect day for a drive through the English countryside. A dazzling sun shines down upon the green fields and hills of the shire of Somerset.

"*Oh, to be in England now that April's come,*" Charles softly intones.

"Tennyson?" Peter asks. "Are you quoting Tennyson?"

"Close," Allie says, "Browning."

"Oh, yes," Peter says. Then he offers up some Browning himself: "*Childe Roland to the dark tower came,*" he says.

"I'm impressed, my lad," Charles remarks, sounding a little like the professor whom they'd left sound asleep back at the hotel. They hadn't chosen to rouse Professor Wentworth when the three of them had gone down for breakfast, and he was still deep in his slumbers when they'd returned to the room. So Charles left him a quickly scrawled note: "Taking Peter back to his school. Don't wait for us for lunch. We'll see you later in the day." The professor wasn't the only one they'd be seeing later in the day; members of the Avon & Somerset Constabulary were eager to hear all about their experiences of the night before and would be talking with them at 3 p.m.

"Do you like football, Peter?" Charles says, searching for a benign topic of conversation. He turns and looks over his shoulder at the boy seated behind him in Allie's car. The three of them are now ten miles into the drive from Glastonbury to the small village in Dorset where Peter's public school is located.

"Oh, yes sir, I do. This year, I'm on the first eleven. Last year I played mostly on defense, but this year I'm center-forward. I've scored a goal in each of our first three matches."

"Well done, Peter," Allie exclaims. "Sounds like you're on your way to being the next Harry Kane!"

The boy chuckles, pleased by her flattery; but Charles notices that he doesn't deny the possibility, either.

"Do you have a favorite Premier League team?" Charles asks.

"Tottenham," the boy replies, "definitely Tottenham."

"Is that the area where your family lives, Peter?" Allie asks.

"Sort of," he replies. "I'm a north London kid."

"Ah, the Tottenham Hotspurs," Charles says. 'Speaking of Harry Kane, Peter, are you familiar with Harry Hotspur?"

"No, sir, can't say that I am. Is he a football player?"

"He's a character from a Shakespeare play," Allie says.

"Oh, right," Peter exclaims, "I know the play you mean. That's the one with Prince Hal and Falstaff. We saw it at Stratford on our school trip. I must say, it's a jolly good play."

"That's the one, Peter," Charles says. "And you're right, it's one of the Bard's best."

"'*The better part of valor is discretion*'," Allie declaims, causing the boy to chuckle again.

As they drive along in silence, Charles enjoys looking at the delightful English countryside of Somerset and taking in all the names on the signs for the villages and little rivers they pass near. At one point they cross the River Brue, and just after that Charles notices a sign for the village of Bruton.

"Bruton," he says. "There's a church in Virginia named after that village."

"And Peter," Allie asks, "do you know who Virginia is named after?"

"No, miss, I can't say that I do."

"The other Queen Elizabeth, the first one, the Virgin Queen."

"Ah, I see," he says. "Well, I shall remember that."

"Are you familiar with Sir Walter Raleigh, Peter? I believe he usually gets credit for naming Virginia."

"Oh, the chap who put his cloak down over the mud puddle so the Queen could keep her feet dry?"

"Yes," Allie says, "that's the fellow."

Half an hour later they're approaching their destination. "Nearly there," Peter says. "When we get there, you can just let me out at the porter's lodge."

"Might we come in and see your school?" Allie asks. "I'd like to do that, if it's okay for non-family members to visit. Your school reminds me quite a lot of the school I once went to."

"It's nothing very special, miss," he says. "Nothing like Eton or anything."

"Does the house in which you live have a particular name?" Allie asks.

"Oh, yes. My house is called The Knoll. I'm a 'Knollie.' There are two other houses—Elmtree and Hillcrest."

❖

Professor Wentworth has missed the breakfast service at the hotel. He stands for a moment in the hotel lobby wondering what he should do when he sees Eva emerge from one of the small rooms just off the lobby.

"Evangeline," he says, "fancy joining me for a bite? I'm just about to set off in search of sustenance."

"Yes, sir, I'll happily join you. They say The Good Earth serves up quite a nice Sunday brunch. Like to give it a try?'

Others obviously have had the same idea and the small restaurant is already crowded when they enter, but they manage to snag the last available table. Soon they've filled their plates with fruit, toast, and eggs.

"I'd just finished my chat with the police when you saw me," Eva says.

"Ah. Tell me about it."

"They wanted to know why we were in the church last night and wanted me to describe exactly what we saw and did. Of course, they asked about the man whose body we found. Did I know him? Did I know where he's from? Did I know who his friends were? Things like that. They actually fingerprinted me (strictly routine, they said). But sir, I was disappointed they didn't confiscate my passport or instruct not to leave the country. All they did was take my contact information in Oxford and say they might need to talk to me again at some point. I was hoping they'd cuff me and read me my rights, but no such luck. I wondered who I would call with my one phone call. I couldn't think of anyone off hand." Eva is smiling.

"You're being too whimsical, Eva," the professor says with a smile that echoes hers.

They look up and see a man now approaching their table. It's Dr. Xander.

"Sorry to intrude," he says to them, "but miss, I was wondering about your friend. How is he doing this morning? Better, I hope."

"My friend?" she asks.

"Dennis? Dennis Adams? I noticed the two of you together at the picnic yesterday and assumed you were friends. Please excuse me, if I'm mistaken."

"Oh, no, you aren't mistaken, Dennis and I are friends. But what do you mean you were wondering how he's doing? Did something happen? Is something wrong?"

"Well, then I guess you don't know. A little lad and I found him lying unconscious in the hotel corridor last night. The poor fellow was badly concussed. They wanted, quite rightly, to keep him overnight in the hospital for observation."

"Goodness," the professor says. "Do you have any idea what happened?"

"No, but it looked to me like he might have sustained some kind of blow to the back of his head."

"An accident?" the professor asks.

Dr. Xander shrugs. "Hard to say."

Eva's face has turned pale. "Gosh, I think I had better go and check on Dennis," she says, standing up. "Sorry to desert you, professor."

"Go, Eva, go. And please do let me know what you find out."

"I'm sorry to be the bearer of bad news," Dr. Xander says.

"Oh, no. Thank you for telling me," Eva says. "You've been most kind." Then she scurries across the room and out the door.

❖

When George Harpole awakens late on Sunday morning in his hotel room, he immediately senses that something is wrong. Despite his raging hangover, he has a vague recollection of having seen Nadja last night, of her coming to him in the bar and giving him a warning. His unease is abetted by Geoff's absence and by his realization that Geoff's bed hasn't been slept in. Geoff didn't return to the room last night, that much is obvious. Then George vaguely recalls Nadja saying that things at the church "would be bad." George hadn't known what she meant. Could something "bad" have happened to Geoff at the church? George doesn't want to know.

What should he do? He's wrestling with that question when there comes a loud knocking on his door. It's the police.

❖

Allie, Charles, and Peter drive alongside a high brick wall enclosing a cluster of buildings.

"That's The Knoll over there," the boy says, pointing toward a two-story building on a small rise a couple hundred yards away. "But we'll need to go in through the main gate."

Allie pulls to a stop in a parking area before the porter's lodge, and they all pile out. Peter carries his jacket and haversack, all he'd taken with him to Glastonbury.

"Master Saunders," the porter says to Peter, with a nod.

"These are my friends, Bates. They want to see the school. Mr. Bascombe is an American."

"Welcome, Sir and Madam," he says with a hint of a smile. "Enjoy the tour."

"Thank you, Mr. Bates," Charles says.

"No," the man replies, "it's just Bates."

First off, Peter leads them to The Knoll, his house of residence. His tiny room boasts a small single bed and an ancient-looking wooden desk that's been shoved beneath the room's one window; there's a bedside table with a clock and a reading lamp. A clutter of books fill two long wall shelves above the bed. Posters of football players adorn the other walls. Charles thinks the boy's cherished possessions do a lot to alleviate the feel of the room being a prison cell.

Charles glances at the posters: "Tottenham Spurs, of course," he says, "no surprise there."

"Peter," Allie says, "that's a nice view from your window. Oh, and there's a croquette lawn down there."

She runs her eye over the titles of the boy's books and says, "Kipling and Conan Doyle. Ah, Philip Pullman. Excellent choices, Peter."

"I quite like all of those writers, miss," the boy replies.

After showing them his room and leaving off his haversack,

Peter leads them on a tour that includes the chapel, the assembly hall, the dining hall, and the students' common room. Few other students are about on this quiet Sunday morning.

Then he takes them out to the sports fields, paying particular attention to the football pitch, obviously his pride and joy. "We have a match next Friday at Shaftsbury," he says.

"Is Shaftsbury good? Will it be a tough one?" Allie asks.

"They're all tough, but Shaftesbury's undefeated," he says. "Still, if we play our best, we should have a chance."

Charles nods, indicating his approval of the boy's sentiments.

"Peter, might we take you to lunch?" Allie asks him as they are winding up the little tour. "Is there a tearoom in the village that you especially like?"

"Oh, miss, I can just eat here. They'll be serving Sunday dinner to the boys who've stayed for the weekend. You've already treated me to last night's supper and to breakfast this morning."

"I have to say that, after the drive and the tour, I'm feeling a bit famished myself," Charles says. "Peter, please do join us. It might be our last chance to visit with you."

The boy, who's already begun to feel sad about the impending departure of his new friends, is readily talked into it. And, in fact, he does know of "quite a nice place in the village" that offers an assortment of soups, sandwiches, and salads—it's called The Three Compasses.

Seated in the tearoom, Charles runs his eyes over the décor of the main room. The small, square tables are covered with white cloths arranged cattycorner over red ones. The wallshelves are jammed with bric-a-brac—commemorative plates, old bottles, ships' bells, and a few other nautical-looking items.

The after-church crowd hasn't appeared yet and there are only a few other diners in the room. A teenaged girl scribbles their orders on her pad, then scurries off to the kitchen.

"You've been here before, then?" Allie asks Peter.

"Twice, actually. Once with my mother, and another time when our sports master brought the first eleven here for a post-match treat."

"Do you have siblings, Peter?" Allie asks him.

"A sister. She's five years older. Studying Languages at Exeter."

"Good university," Allie says, "and nice that she's not far away. Where do you think you might go when the time comes?"

"Haven't given it much thought, miss."

"Oxford or Cambridge, perhaps?" Charles asks.

"Don't know about that, sir. Don't know if I could get in or if my father could afford it."

"Your father," Allie says, "what does he do?"

"North Sea oil. He's so busy we don't really see much of him." Peter fiddles nervously with one of his spoons.

"Does he work out on one of those big oil rigs?" Ally asks.

"Oh no. He's in management. But their main office is on the coast nearby in Scotland. That's where he stays most of the time."

Charles, sensing that the boy isn't comfortable with this topic, says, "I guess you like History quite a lot, Peter. Is it your favorite subject?"

"I do love History, though I love literature just about as much."

"At dinner last night," Allie said, "you mentioned that you saw the replicas of the lances in the church and found them fascinating. I have to say that I did, too."

"Umm," Peter says, working up his nerve, "about those lances, there's something I probably should confess."

They look at him expectantly, waiting for him to go on.

"When I was in there looking at them yesterday, something very odd happened." Peter still fiddles nervously with his spoon.

"What was that, Peter?" Allie asks. "Want to tell us about it?"

"Well . . . I think I may have done something I shouldn't have done."

Charles and Allie sit quietly, offering him encouraging looks.

"You see, I knew I wasn't supposed to be in the church. I saw the sign saying that it was closed . . . but I went in anyway."

"So did we, Peter," Allie says. "We didn't mean any harm, and I'm sure you didn't either."

"As I was in there looking at the lances," the boy goes on, "I heard someone else come in and heard them walking toward where I was. I didn't know what they might do if they found me, so . . . well . . . I hid." Then the boy pauses in his story.

"That was a smart thing to do, Peter," Allie says. "They might have given you a good scolding, an undeserved scolding."

"Any idea who it was?" Charles asks. "Did you find out

what they were doing there?"

"I couldn't see the person because I'd hidden myself behind one of the cases. But I listened carefully, and you know what? That bloke, well, it sounded to me like he was *hiding* something."

"My word," Allie says.

"And what do you think he was hiding?" Charles asks. "Were you able to discover the hiding place?"

"From behind the case, I couldn't see *exactly* what he was doing, but I waited until after he was gone. Then I went and investigated. He'd jammed something into a narrow space behind one of the other cases. He left, never knowing I was there. After he was gone, I went and retrieved what he'd hidden. It was a small box."

"But you didn't take it, did you?" Charles asks.

"Oh, sir, of *course* I didn't take it." Peter sounds rather offended at the idea that he would do such a thing.

"No, of course you didn't," Allie says, trying to smooth the lad's ruffled feathers. She gives Charles the side-eye. "Did you open the box and see what was in it?"

The boy nods. "Yes, I did. And then I did something else—something I maybe shouldn't have done."

"And what was that?" Charles asks.

"I didn't take the box, sir, but what I did do was change its location. I moved it just a bit from its original hiding place to another place."

"Why did you do that, Peter?" Allie asks.

"I only meant it as a little joke, miss. I mean, my goodness, that fellow had given me quite a fright. Right then it seemed to me only fair that I return the favor. I wanted to give him a fright when he came back for it and couldn't find it right off."

"Yes," Charles says, "that sounds perfectly reasonable to me. I think I might've done the same thing."

"And besides, I left it where he could easily find it, practically in plain sight. Really easy to find. Honestly, I didn't mean any harm."

"Of course, you didn't," Allie says. "And the place you shifted it to, Peter—that wouldn't be the top of one of the lance cases, would it?"

Astonishment appears on Peter's and Charles' faces at the same time.

"Miss," Peter says, "how could you know that?"

Allie reaches into her handbag and pulls something out. There, cradled in her hand, lies a small wooden box with a hinged lid. "This wouldn't be the box by any chance?"

"That looks like the one! How did you get it?" Wide-eyed, he stares at her; Charles does too.

"Quite easily," Allie says—"by snatching it off the top of the case where you must've placed it."

Charles and the boy sit in stunned silence.

"My word," the boy finally says.

"Holy Jerusalem," Charles says. "And why did you do that?"

"Just a sudden impulse, I guess. Something had caught my eye, something I hadn't noticed when we were there the night before. Peter," Allie goes on, "do you have any idea what's in the box?"

"No, miss. At least, I'm not entirely sure. I did take a quick peek at it, though."

"Why don't we all have a good look at it now, shall we?" Allie raises the hinged lid, and they gaze upon a small cloth bag nestled inside the little box.

Allie pulls out the bag and loosens a draw string. She opens the mouth of the bag and carefully extracts an object which she then places back down atop the bag on the table.

The three of them gaze upon a sharp-pointed metal object. It's been fitted onto a piece of smooth wood. The whole thing is no more than about seven or eight inches in length. The metal is dull looking but not rusted. Its tip is blacker than the rest. Dried blood? Charles wonders.

"A spear-tip?" Allie muses aloud. "Or perhaps a very good replica of a spear-tip?"

"I studied all the replicas of the holy lances quite carefully," Peter says. "One of them was missing its tip. I'll have it in my notes, back in my room."

"Peter," Charles says, "your recollection is absolutely correct. The one that's missing its tip is the holy lance in the Vatican."

"Yes, yes," Peter says, "that's the one!"

The three of them sit there quietly now, each of them pondering the questions that have shot into their minds.

"Maybe," Peter says, "that fellow who came in and frightened me had stolen it from its case, then decided to bring it back. But if so, why had he hidden it? He had a perfect chance to return it to its case right then. Hmm."

"Maybe the case was locked," Allie suggests. "And, since

he couldn't return it, he decided to leave it close by in a spot where it wouldn't be noticed."

"Anyway," Charles says, "Allie and I had better get it back to Glastonbury and place this matter in the hands of professionals. When we find out the answers, Peter, we'll be sure to let you know. And maybe we can tell you in person. That is, if you'd be interested in having a visit to Oxford."

"Come to Oxford? Oh, sir, I would love to come to Oxford. Really? Could I do that?"

Allie was beaming a look of approval at Charles.

"If it's okay with your mother, Peter," Charles says. 'But you will have to get her permission. Actually, she could come as well."

"I don't think she'd be interested," Peter says, "but I'll ask her. Anyway, I'm sure she'll give her approval. Oh, my, a visit to Oxford would be splendid."

"And I'm sure the professor would enjoy showing you around the city," Charles says. "He knows Oxford's secrets much better than I do."

"Almost as well as Lyra does in Philip Pullman," Allie says with a smile.

"Will you come, too, miss?" Peter asks hopefully.

"I will if I'm invited," she says.

"Invited?" Charles says. "I was thinking you would be the one hosting the shindig."

"In that case, Peter, I shall certainly be there."

"Do you like dogs, Peter?" Charles asks. "I'm sure Mrs. Hawkins, my landlady, would like it if you were willing to walk her Dalmatian named Agnes."

"I'd like that, sir. I've wanted to have a dog, but my father wouldn't allow it.'

CHAPTER 15

—"The Better Part of Valor"—

When Allie and Charles are a few miles into the drive back to Glastonbury, Allie says, "I'm glad we'll be staying in touch with Peter. He's a delightful lad."

"I can't help but smile at his rationale for moving the lance point," Charles says. "It's like something I might've done myself when I was his age."

"You boys and your codes," Allie says, half-mockingly.

"Girls don't do things like that?"

"Oh yes, they certainly do. But girls don't have pangs of conscience about it."

"Actually," Charles says, "your rationale for stuffing it in your handbag makes me smile as well."

"I really can't explain why I did that," Allie replies. "It was just a sudden impulse. I'm sure you've acted on sudden impulses. Everyone does."

Charles thinks about it for a moment. "Yes . . . well, . . . I have done that . . . but just once that I can remember."

"Just *once*? And when was that?"

"It was about a year ago, actually—that time when, all of a sudden I . . . fell for you."

"*Fell* for me? You fell for *me*? Well, goodness, my dear

sir, I guess that proves my point—sometimes having a sudden impulse can be quite a good thing." She reaches out her free hand and gives Charles' shoulder a little squeeze.

They drive on in silence for another minute before Allie says, "Charlie, what do you suppose the object in the box really is?"

He ponders her question for a long moment before answering. "I'd say it's one of two things. It's a replica of the missing lance point, as you and Peter both suggested at lunch; or, . . . it isn't."

"And if it isn't?"

"If it isn't, . . . then it just might not be a replica."

"Meaning that it might be the *real thing?*"

"Yes, that's what I mean. Seems incredibly unlikely, but yes."

" . . . wow. Charlie, if it's the real thing, then it would be a physical object that actually came into contact with the body of Jesus Christ."

"Yes—which would make it one of the holiest and most precious objects in all of Christendom."

Another minute goes by as each of them is lost in their own thoughts.

"What do you think we should do?" Allie finally says.

"You mean after we've sold it to the Pope? Maybe sail around the world in our brand-new luxury yacht?"

"No, silly goose. What should we do when we get back to Glastonbury?"

"Ah, you're thinking *short*-term, I was thinking *long*-term."

"Whom do we tell? And what do we tell them? What do we do with this object we have in our possession? Tell Albert and Edwin? Tell the police when we speak with them this afternoon? Or . . . tell nobody at all?"

"Hmm. Let's reflect on the matter before we decide. One thing I do know—we *don't* let Bright-Rogers and his pals know about it. Those guys have got to be involved in all of this in one fashion or another."

"And not in a good fashion."

"No, probably not."

"Charlie," Allie asks, her fingers drumming on the steering wheel, "you don't think we're murder suspects, do you?"

"Seriously, *us*?"

"Yes—you, me, the professor, and Eva. We were the first ones on the scene. We're the ones who found the body."

"Allie, that would be crazy. Two well-respected, upstanding young women, and a pair of dusty, old English professors!"

"You're not so old, Charlie," she replies, "though I won't cavil about 'dusty.'"

"Ha, ha, neither will I."

A moment later a sign to the village of Cerne Abbas catches Charles' eye. He can't help smiling at the name, which triggers a certain association in his mind.

"Allie, have you ever seen the Cerne Abbas Giant?"

Allie laughs. "We prefer to call him the Cerne Abbas *man*. He caused me and my school friends much mirth when our teacher took us to see him."

"One of Britain's most celebrated chalk figures," Charles

says, still smiling.

"Oh, yes, celebrated all right—especially on May Day when all the young girls go up the hill and decorate his you-know-what with wreaths of flowers. The origin of the May Pole. Want to stop and have a look?"

"No, maybe we'd better not. Might make me feel a bit, umm, inadequate."

Allie hesitates before offering a reply. Finally, she says, "No worries there, Charlie."

After another fifteen minutes into the drive, they get their first sight of Glastonbury Tor. "Wow," Charles says, "you can actually see the Tor from a good twenty miles away."

"Oh, yes. On a clear day, you can even see it from atop the ancient hillfort at Cadbury Castle. Something I've done. That's a distance of at least twenty-five miles."

"Listen, if we were to go and pick up Peter to take him for his visit to Oxford," Charles says, "maybe we could stop at Cadbury. It would be on our way. Then Peter could actually say he'd been to 'Camelot.' "

"A splendid idea, Charlie. I really do like that young lad. And Charlie, he really likes you. But did you have the sense that there's some tension between him and his father?"

"Sounded to me like his father is pretty much an absent father."

"To me, too. Kind of sad. There's always been some tension between me and my mum, but Daddy and I have always been very close."

"Yes—and he even taught you to play darts!" Charles says. He thinks about a memorable evening nearly a year earlier when the two them engaged in a darts match in a pub in Cornwall, a darts match that practically became a life-or-death matter.

"Darts among other things. So, how about you and *your* father?" Allie asks, hopefully. It's been a rare occasion when she's succeeded in prying information out of Charles about himself, his family, or his life in America.

"My dad? Well, he wanted me to be a football player—*American* football, not some sissy European game. But he was out of luck. Had to be satisfied with a basketball, baseball-playing son, something he grudgingly came to terms with. Later on, after I got my Ph.D., he took great satisfaction in beating me in Scrabble."

"He beat you?"

"Most of the time. He'd learned all those sneaky little words with q's and z's. Believe me, he was a guy you wouldn't want to play poker with. He'd put you in the poor house with no hesitation, no qualms."

"But you could beat him in cribbage?"

"There I held my own. It was probably about fifty-fifty."

As they approach Glastonbury, Charles notices Allie is once more drumming her fingers nervously on the steering wheel. s.

"Charles," Allie says, her voice anything but calm, "what *dummies* we are!"

"Dummies? I know we're dummies, generally speaking. But do you have something more specific in mind?"

"Charlie, haven't you realized that you and I could be in danger? Hasn't it dawned on you? Charlie, that man who was murdered last night was murdered for a *reason*. His body was arranged the way it was for a *reason*. Don't you think it must have to do with the missing spear-tip? Whoever did all that was looking for the spear-tip—the spear-tip you and I now have in our possession! Charlie, we could be next. He, or they, could be looking for us right this minute."

"Allie, come on. We don't know for certain why that man was murdered."

"Hah."

"And anyway, how could anyone know we have the spear-tip? Anyone other than you, me, and Peter. Even the professor and Eva don't know that. *I* didn't know it until a couple of hours ago—when the thing strangely materialized inside your handbag. You may be right that a lot of these events are connected to the spear-tip. But I don't see how you and I can be in any immediate danger."

Allie, listening to his words, had a doubtful look on her face. "Charlie, you and I are in danger because *we* are the ones who have the spear-tip. That's the simple fact of the matter."

"What we need to do, I would suggest," Charles says, "is do nothing to call attention to ourselves. We go about things as we normally would. Even so, I don't want you to be the one holding on to the artifact. So, listen here, baby (doing his best, though not very good, imitation of Humphrey Bogart) —fork it over, or I'll have to wring your slender, sexy neck!"

"Not funny, Charlie. Listen, don't you think we should at

least tell Albert and Edwin?"

"Well, maybe. But what I'd like to do first, now I think about it, is show it to the Curator of Ancient Artifacts at the Ashmolean, a man named Oliver-John Oldhouse. He's a close chum of the professor, a true professional and, according to the professor, a man of absolute integrity—not some sleezy bastard like Nigel Bright-Rogers. And as for Albert and Edwin, what gives me pause about telling them is the fact that those two fellows work for the government."

"You don't trust the government?"

It was Charles' turn to say, "Hah. You mean you do?"

"In general, no. But Albert and Edwin? Come on, Charlie, they're cribbage players. If you can't trust cribbage players, who can you trust?"

"You can trust me, you, and Peter," Charles says firmly.

"That's it? That's the whole list? Not even the professor?"

"Well, okay, and the professor. And maybe the guy at the Ashmolean."

"Just maybe?"

"Well . . . probably."

OXFORD

CHAPTER 15

— The Ashmolean Museum—

By Monday morning, the story of a grisly crucifixion-style murder in a church in Glastonbury is front page news all across the U.K. The British tabloids—especially *The Sun*, *The Daily Mail*, and *The Daily Mirror*—try to out-do each other, each one attempting to make the tale more lurid than their rivals. *The Mirror*, somehow, has even managed to come up with a photograph of the body all laid out on the prayer chapel floor. (Perhaps, Charles thinks, it's come courtesy of a policeman wishing to pick up a few extra pounds). The accounts in *The Times*, *The Guardian*, and *The Daily Telegraph* are more circumspect, but the story still merits front-page coverage.

According to the newspapers, the police have no one in custody and no suspects, but they are interviewing several persons of interest. They also posit a possible connection to a similar death that occurred six weeks earlier in the city of Hull, a death that involved a young woman, a museum worker, who'd recently emigrated from Poland.

As he sips his morning coffee, Charles reads the account in *The Times*. They have the bare facts correct, he thinks, and they do mention that an academic conference focusing on the Holy

Grail had been occurring in Glastonbury over the weekend. He's relieved, however, to see that there's no mention of the replicas of the lances that were on display in the church. Maybe the police didn't think it was relevant; or maybe they omitted that fact intentionally in their comments to the press. One new thing Charles does learn, though, is that the dead man was killed by a blow to the head; the "crucifixion" scenario was merely window dressing.

Charles sets the newspaper aside and refills his coffee cup. He sits for a moment at his desk staring out the front window at the expanse of lawn Mrs. Hawkins calls her "garden." He's been mowing it for her ever since he first rented the flat nearly a year ago, and he knows she likes to have the grass kept short. It's begun to look a bit shaggy, so he should probably have a go at it later this afternoon after the meeting he and the professor will have with the professor's friend at the Ashmolean Museum.

❖

At ten a.m. on Monday morning, Allie Tremayne opens the art gallery where she works in St. Ives and goes into her usual routine. She knows that her boss, Mrs. Marchand, the gallery owner, won't be in before eleven, but that she'd better have the coffee ready for her when she shows up. No potential customers are waiting by the front door when Allie comes in, and it looks like she'll have a quiet morning. It's still a month before the tourist season *really* heats up, but the quaint little town of St. Ives, with its beaches, harbor, art galleries, and museums, is popular all year 'round.

On the long, solitary drive back from Glastonbury in the

late afternoon yesterday, Allie had time to reflect on quite a lot of things. Heading the list, of course, were the horrific events of Saturday night. Fortunately, those recollections had been muted somewhat by their little jaunt to Peter's school, which had been an enjoyable interlude.

Her thoughts also return to the conversation she'd had with Professor Wentworth at the hotel on Saturday night, before all hell broke loose at the church. How much of a future did she really want to have with Charles? The more she thinks about the possibility of going to America with him, the more it begins to feel like something she really wants to do—but only if it's something *he* really wants her to do. She reflects on her desire to pursue a career as a serious painter. If she does focus all her energies on becoming a painter of note, and she believes she does want to attempt that, being in America with Charles might enhance her chances of achieving her goal. But most of all, she very much desires to be together with Charles, in one fashion or another. What she needs now is for Charles to show that he's as enthusiastic about it as she is.

Maybe, she thinks, she needs to give him a good nudge in that direction, a hefty little poke in the ribs.

❖

Since it's another lovely April day, Charles decides to walk the nearly two miles from Summertown to the center of Oxford. He strides quickly down the busy Woodstock Road toward the Center, but even so, it takes him half an hour to reach the Eagle & Child pub in St. Giles Street. It's exactly 1:30 when he steps through the door. He sees Professor Wentworth already seated at a table, finishing a piece of apple pie and drinking a cup of coffee. A handful of others of the mid-day crowd still linger in the pub, including a few American tourists who have come there to experience the ambiance of a place once regularly frequented by C.S. Lewis and his fellow Inklings.

Professor Wentworth has arranged a 2 p.m. meeting at the Ashmolean with his old college friend, Oliver-John Oldhouse, the museum's Curator of Ancient Artifacts. Charles and the professor want to strategize a bit prior to that meeting. The professor looks up from his coffee as Charles enters. "Punctual, as usual," he says, with a smile.

"It was a bit nerve-racking, sir, but fortunately I didn't encounter any muggers."

"Muggers in Oxford, Charlie? Never in Oxford. Though what they would have made of the object I assume you have in your backpack would be worth knowing."

"Totally bummed out, no doubt. But they would have snagged a fine umbrella, half an egg salad sandwich, and a San Diego Padres windbreaker, not to mention the highly service-able backpack itself."

"Quite a haul, Charlie."

The waitress has overheard this little exchange but thinks nothing of it. She's used to hearing her customers exchanging peculiar remarks. This is Oxford.

"Would you bring this lad a slice of the apple pie?" the professor says. "Oh, and while you're at it, why not bring me another." When they are alone again he says, "Well, Charlie, I assume you do have it with you?"

"Oh, yes. Kind of thrilling, not to say nerve-racking, to be walking about with a backpack containing what might be one of the most precious Christian artifacts in existence."

After the waitress brings their pie, Charles says, "So, sir, mind telling me more about this man we'll be seeing?"

"His name, as you already know, is Oliver-John Oldhouse, and as you also already know, he's the Curator of Ancient Artifacts at the Ashmolean Museum. His underlings, of course, refer to him as O.J., though never directly to his face. He wouldn't care too much for that; he's quite a strait-laced fellow. Oliver-John and I go way back. We were at Merton together, along with Allie's father, though he and Allie's father were *not* good friends—like oil and water, those two— Oliver-John too much the stuffy, snobbish English academic for Celtic-loving Rhys Tremaine. But Oliver-John and I got along quite well. Indeed, we were on Merton's First Eight together, me rowing stroke, he our cockswain. We made a fine team. He was, and is, a wily little fox, one very bright fellow."

"Like you, sir, I believe he has established a reputation as one of Oxford's most distinguished scholars."

"He's as capable as they come, Charlie, and most important for our purposes, a man of impeccable integrity. Not like Nigel Bright-Rogers—even though Oliver-John had a hand in training that slippery bugger."

"So, the plan is that we simply show him the artifact and innocently solicit his opinion about what it might be? We offer no hints about what *we* suspect it might be?"

"Quite right. He'll probably see through us right off, knowing that we aren't quite the innocent babes we're passing ourselves off as being. But I have no doubt that he will be able to give us some valuable suggestions about how we might proceed. If it begins to look like we have what we think we could have, Oliver-John might even volunteer to get personally involved. It would be something he'd want to see handled honestly and correctly. And he would be a most useful ally to have in various kinds of negotiations. He knows a great many well-placed people."

Oxford's Ashmolean Museum, Britain's first public museum, lies in the heart of the city on Beaumont Street, just across from the Randolph Hotel and half a block from the Martyrs Monument at the south end of St. Giles Street. The Ashmolean dates originally to the 17th Century when Elias Ashmole bequeathed his "Cabinet of Curiosities" to Oxford University. The present building was erected in the 19th Century and re-modeled in the 21st. Charles knows that the museum's many collections include ancient artifacts from Egypt and Greece as well as a variety of Viking and Anglo-Saxon treasures. The Fine Art wings feature paintings and drawings by a host of famous artists—e.g., Constable, Sargent, Manet, Renoir, Van Gogh, Picasso, and Cezanne. The collection of Pre-Raphaelite paintings is especially notable.

At the entrance, Charles and Professor Wentworth show the museum's security guards the object they'd been forewarned about. Then they proceed upstairs to the corridor housing the administrative offices. Oliver-John Oldhouse's Personal Assistant welcomes them and ushers them into his office. They accept her offer of coffee.

As Charles looks across the desk at the small bespectacled man with the neatly trimmed beard and reddish hair interspersed with gray, he imagines him forty years earlier as the cockswain of the Merton College First Eight. The man still looks fit enough to do it today. The professor introduces Charles, and then the two old friends exchange pleasantries until the young woman arrives with the coffee.

"So, Charles," Oldhouse says, "William tells me you've stumbled upon something you'd like me to look at and offer an opinion on. I'm happy to do that, if what you have falls anywhere within my expertise." He pauses and stares expectantly at Charles.

"Oh, yes," Charles says. He roots about in his backpack and pulls out the object that's he's wrapped inside his windbreaker. He extracts the small wooden box and places it down on the man's desk. Oldhouse takes his time opening it. Then he studies the object for a long moment without comment.

"And what do you make of it, William?" Oldhouse asks Professor Wentworth.

"Well, it appears to both of us that it might be the metal point of a weapon of some sort, perhaps a spear or a lance. We've been wondering about its age and also about its possible origins. Charles and I are strictly literature people, Oliver-John. Beyond medieval manuscripts, our knowledge of the material culture of the Middle Ages isn't extensive."

The man lifts the object and turns it slowly in his hands. "This may not be medieval," he says. Charles notices that he only handles the wooden shaft of the object while studying the weapon's point most carefully.

"Gentlemen, might I ask you how this most intriguing object happened to come into your possession?"

The professor doesn't reply but glances toward Charles as if to say, "How about you fielding that one."

"Uh, well, sir . . . it just sort of fell into the lap of a friend of ours."

"Not my old acquaintance Rhys Tremaine, I hope. He of the mysterious Chaucer manuscripts."

"Ha, ha," laughs the professor. "No, not this time. Nothing to do with Rhys this time."

"No, well, I suppose not. Rhys is strictly antiquarian books, isn't he? Never touches anything in this line."

"Quite," the professor replies.

"And, I don't suppose it has anything to do with that conference in Glastonbury on the Holy Grail that occurred this past weekend? A conference where some poor chap went and got himself killed?"

"Not so far as I know," the professor replies. "But I must confess that Charles and I, sadly, were two of the ones who discovered the man's body. Bloody awful experience."

"No doubt, no doubt," he says, looking at them with big eyes.

"So, sir," Charles says, "how do you think we should proceed? Do you have any advice for us?"

"Yes . . . perhaps I do. William, Charles, would you chaps be willing to run it past Jonathon Owens over at the Pitt-Rivers. See if he might get his scientists to run some tests on it? Would that be all right? Then Jon might be able to give us an approximation of its age."

"Ah, I know Jon Owens," the professor says, "a most capable chap. Yes, Oliver-John, that seems an excellent idea."

"Then I'll give him a call, shall I? See if we can't find a time that's mutually agreeable?"

"I would appreciate that, sir," Charles says. "And do you think he might be able to determine if that's dried blood on the metal end of the thing?"

"Yes, I think it's likely he'll be able to do that."

❖

"Peter, did you hear about the murder in Glastonbury?" Dickie, Peter's closest friend, sounds excited. "Just two days after we were there!"

Peter hasn't heard about it. But now all the boys in his history class are buzzing about it. One of them has a copy of the *Daily Mirror* with the gruesome photo. "Look at that!" he cries out. He passes the newspaper around, and Peter can't help staring with fascination at the body stretched out on the floor of the little chapel, a little chapel in which he himself had spent an hour or two just a few days earlier.

The photo excites Peter. He wonders who the man could be. He hadn't been able to get a view of the fellow who had frightened him so much when he'd hidden behind the display case. Maybe this is *him*.

Peter hasn't told anyone about the day he spent in Glastonbury alone, not even Dickie, his best friend. He decides that for now, anyway, he'd better keep mum about it. He wonders if his American friend in Oxford and the nice woman named Allie have heard about the murder. He feels sure that by now they must have. Anyway, he'll ask them when he sees them. He doesn't know when that will be, but he hopes it will be soon. A visit to Oxford, he thinks, would be smashing.

"Peter? Day-dreaming?" comes the voice of his teacher. "Not like you to be inattentive. So let me repeat my question. Could you give me the date and the location of the signing of the Magna Carta?"

"Sorry, sir, Yes, let me see. The Magna Carta was signed in 1215 . . . at . . . Runnymede, which is close to Windsor."

"Yes, quite right. Dickie, can you tell us who the involved parties were?"

"Oh, sir," says another boy, "I've seen one of the original copies of the Magna Carta, at Salisbury Cathedral."

"Please don't interrupt, Michael. Please wait until you are called upon."

❖

Charles feels relieved, knowing that the object is now in responsible, professional hands. It's been a harrowing couple of days. Maybe he can finally relax a bit and re-focus his attention on the scholarly project he'd interrupted to head off to Glastonbury.

But, thinking that an additional ounce of prevention might be a good thing, too, Charles decides to make a short detour before hiking back to North Oxford from the Bodleian Library where he's been working. His footsteps soon lead him toward the slightly down-at-the-heels section of Oxford known as Jericho.

A couple of minutes later Charles enters the "Ye Olde AN-TI-QUES Shoppe," an ancient institution he's poked about in a couple of times before. Charles has a nodding acquaintance with the old fellow behind the counter, a man who recognizes the American from his previous visits.

"Ah, welcome, sir. I remember you buyin' that Oxford United jersey a while back."

"Yes. I sent it to a pal of mine who plays recreational soccer back in the States."

'Lookin' for anyt'ing in particular today?" the man asks.

Charles has moved to the section of the shop where there's a jumble of old musical instruments.

"Yes," Charles says, "any old brass instruments, trumpets or cornets? Ah, I see one." Charles reaches for a beat-up-looking cornet and then brings it to his lips. The mouthpiece is still in it, and Charles blows a few breaths through the instrument to warm it up. Then he sounds a single note, holding for it for several seconds, before slowly playing a scale from low C to high C. He plays the scale a second time, this time adding in all the flats and sharps. He does it once more, this time obligato.

"Well done, sir," the old geezer says. "'Nother week, you'll be sounding just like John Coltrane hisself."

"No, I really doubt that," Charles says.

"Why not, sir, why not? You certainly got the knack."

"Maybe because Coltrane played the sax, not the cornet?" Charles replies.

"Ah. I believe ya got me on that one," the man says, grinning.

Charles sets the cornet on the counter, then picks up an ancient-looking cricket bat.

"Just so's you know, sir, that un's got a slight crack a bit above the handle. Wouldn't want ta sell you no flawed goods."

"That's okay. I don't intend to use it to play. Just want it for a colorful reminder of my time in jolly old England."

"Ah, I got ya, sir."

Beneath the glass top of the counter Charles sees an impressive array of weaponry, mostly knives. In their midst he spots an item that interests him. "Are those brass knuckles you have in there?" he asks.

"Ah, the knuckle dusters. Wicked little buggers. You wouldn't be figgerin' on fightin' someone, now would you, sir?"

"Oh, no. But would you pull them out so I could take a look?"

The man hands them to Charles, who notices the little tag that says, "NOT FOR SALE." Charles slides the fingers of his right hand into the brass knuckles. It's a tight fit but doable. "How much for these?" he asks.

"Ah, no, can't be doin' that. Illegal for me to sell 'em, illegal for you even to have 'em."

"Okay, then," Charles says, "how much for the cornet and cricket bat?"

"Why don't I give you the pair for, say, 35 pound—and I'll throw in some valve oil for the cornet for free. You'll be needin' some of that." Charles nods.

"Sure you won't throw in the brass knuckles, too?"

"Ha, ha . . . no. 'Fraid I can't do that."

Charles looks at the price tags on the two items and they total just 30 pounds, plus another 2 for the value oil. Charles pulls out his wallet and says, "I've got a twenty and a pair of fivers. Would you take thirty for the lot?"

"Ya drive a hard bargain, sir. But since you're payin' cash, yes, I'll take the thirty."

Charles stashes the cricket bat, the valve oil, and the cornet, which has no carrying case, in his backpack, the handle of the cricket bat sticking out of the top.

"Pleasure doing business with you, sir," the man says. "Hope ta see you again soon."

"A pleasure for me, too," Charles replies.

Mrs. Hawkins and Agnes are just setting out for their afternoon walk when Charles comes up the driveway.

"Looks like quite a load, Charlie," she says, spotting the handle of the cricket bat poking up behind his shoulder.

"I've purchased myself a few treasures, Mrs. Hawkins. But I need to forewarn you about one of them. It's a cornet." He removes it from the backpack and holds it before him.

"Charlie, you're a man of hidden talents."

"I'll try to restrict my practicing to the mornings when you're out doing your errands."

"Oh, no need to do that. I'll enjoy hearing your squeaks and squawks."

"But here's the favor I'd like to ask of you. If you ever hear me blow three long, sustained notes—he holds the cornet to his lips and sounds three loud notes to show her—then I want you to call the police immediately."

"Seriously? Call the police?"

"Yes, any time of the day or night, call the police. The cornet and you shall be my warning system."

"Your warning system? Charlie, against what?"

"I really don't know, Mrs. Hawkins. Call it an ounce of prevention."

CHAPTER 16
— Eyes Are Watching You—

George Harpole senses that he's being watched. He has no real evidence of it, but he can't avoid having that feeling every time he leaves his flat.

George wishes he could go back to Glastonbury and try to search out the missing artifact, but he knows he can't do that. Anyway, by now it's probably long gone. But still, he thinks, there's a slight chance no one noticed it when they removed the cases with the lance replicas because the light is always dim inside the small prayer chapel. So, just maybe, it's still there. Should he take a risk and go and see? George had never been much of a risk-taker.

It's probably a lost opportunity, and yet the monetary value of the thing keeps nagging at him. And now, with Geoff a goner, he wouldn't even have to split it with anyone. What a horribly crass and selfish thought, he tells himself. Geoff was his friend.

George's colleagues at Hull have all expressed their sympathies about Geoff's death. And yet after their perfunctory gestures, they all returned quickly to business as usual. Is that what our lives are worth? George wonders. All we do is make a very small ripple on the surface of the water, a small ripple that soon disappears, and then it's as if we were never there at all?

According to the Bard, George thinks, "Our little life is rounded with a sleep." If that's the case, George says to himself, then rest in peace, Geoff. And you, too, Nadja. I shall carry both of your memories with me for the rest of my days. I wonder if anyone will carry mine?

❖

It's late on Tuesday afternoon and Charles, after spending a long day transcribing a text in the Bodleian Library, is trekking up the Banbury Road when he feels his phone vibrate. He stops and perches himself on a low brick wall and checks the number. It's Allie. Charles listens to her message.

"Charlie," her voice says, "something's happened. Call me as soon as you can."

Charles hits reply and Allie immediately answers.

"Allie, what's going on?" he asks.

"Charlie, someone's been in my flat. Charlie, I'm scared." To Charles, she really does sound frightened.

"Oh, man. Are things missing?"

"Not as far as I can tell. But Charlie, I *know* the flat's been searched. A lot of things aren't quite where they would normally be. "

"Allie, you have to get out of there—*now!*"

"And do what?"

"Come here. Tonight. Right now. Throw a few things in an overnight bag and get yourself out of there. You have to come here. And just as quickly as you can get away."

"Charlie, now I've heard your voice, I feel less afraid. And maybe, since they've already searched the place and found nothing, maybe I'll be okay now. Anyway . . . "

"No, Allie, no. You *have* to come. If they think you have the object and couldn't find it in your flat, they might shift their attention to you."

Allie is silent for several seconds. "Okay," she says at last. "I'll need to call Mrs. Marchand, let her know I'll be away for a few days. I'm sure Georgina, my part-time helper, will be happy to fill in for me. I know she can use the extra money."

"Call me once you're in the car and heading for the road. Check your rearview mirror and be sure you aren't being followed. If it seems like there's a car that's been following you closely for a while, once you're on the M5, put the pedal to the metal in that hot little car of yours and let 'em eat your dust. Be as sure as you can that when you turn off the M4 toward Oxford, that it's just you."

Charles heard Allie let out a deep breath. "Okay, I can do all of that. Okay, then, Charlie, look for me in about five hours."

"I can't wait to see you, to put my arms around you, to hold you. Call me if there are any difficulties."

❖

"Charlie," Mrs. Hawkins calls out to him on Wednesday afternoon, as he arrives back at the flat after making a grocery run, "you had visitors today."

"Visitors?"

"Two men. They didn't give their names, but they said they were friends of yours. They didn't ask for Allie, so I didn't mention that she was here inside the flat."

"Thanks, Mrs. H."

"They said they really wanted to see you and that they'd come back later today. Oh, well, here they come now."

Charles watches as two men stroll up the drive. He breathes a sigh of relief as he recognizes Albert and Edwin.

"Bert and Ernie," Charles says with a grin. "Long time, no see."

"Bert and Ernie?" Mrs. Hawkins asks, questioningly.

"Your lodger has a habit of trying to be witty," Albert says.

"And sometimes he is, about halfway," says Edwin.

"Making him a half-wit?" Mrs. Hawkins says.

"My point exactly," Edwin remarks.

"What brings you fine fellas to my humble abode?" Charles asks, ignoring their banter.

"There's something we'd like to show you, if you wouldn't mind obliging us. It's possible you may be able to shed light on some things we don't entirely understand," Edwin says.

"Then come on up. I have a houseguest at the moment, someone you've met before, but I suspect she'll be as pleased to see you as I am. She might even challenge you to a game of cribbage."

"Ah," Albert says, "then it must be that lovely Cornish lass."

"Let me just run up and forewarn her." Charles dashes up the stairs two steps at a time, and the two older men, follow more slowly behind him.

"Charlie, could I bring you all a nice pot of tea?" Mrs. Hawkins calls out. "I can have it ready in a jiffy."

"Yes, Mrs. Hawkins. That would be great. Thanks," Charles calls back.

"Alwyn," Edwin says, as Allie comes into the room. "What a pleasure to see you again. Long way from Cornwall, eh?"

"If Charlie won't come see me, I just have to swallow my pride and go see him," she says.

"Hey, wait a minute," Charles says.

"I think you're teasing the boy," Albert says. "Or you're underestimating the level of his ardor."

"And Albert is a man who knows a thing or two about ardor," Edwin says.

"Indeed," Albert says.

"So, what can we help you with?" Charles asks.

Albert extracts a laptop from his shoulder bag and inserts a thumb drive. "We'd like to show you some footage from a CCTV camera and hear your comments about it. Only takes about fifteen minutes."

"Wow. What's it of?"

"It's from a camera that was mounted over a shop on the High Street in Glastonbury. It offers a partial view of the walkway to St. John's Church. It was the best we could come up with since the church didn't have a security camera of its own. We've edited it down to what we think are the important bits. Why don't we all watch it together, and then maybe you can shed some light on a few things."

Mrs. Hawkins comes in bearing a well-loaded tea tray. "I've brought you an assortment of biscuits," she says. "And for Allie, I included some Jaffa Cakes. She has a weakness for them," she says to Albert and Edwin, adding a wink.

"Yum," says Edwin. "I have a weakness for 'em, too."

Allie pours tea into four cups and the men help themselves to the cookies and the Jaffa Cakes. Allie moves the tea tray over to a sideboard, and then Albert places his opened laptop on the coffee table. A still picture comes up showing the empty walkway leading toward the church. "All set?" Albert asks.

"Let 'er fly," Charles says.

Albert hits play. The scene is empty for a moment and then a boy appears. "It's almost 5 on Saturday afternoon," Albert says. "You can see the time display in the lower right-hand corner of the screen—4:59. Do you know the boy?"

Charles looks at Allie who shrugs.

"Actually," Edwin says, "we know that you do. Later that night we saw you two and the professor come into the hotel along with the boy."

"His name is Peter," Allie says. "On Sunday, we took him back to his school in Dorset."

"We'll probably need to talk to him," Edwin says. "Not that we expect he can tell us a lot."

"I'm sure he'll do his best," Charles says. "He went to the church so he could have a look at the lance replicas on display there. He plans to write a school paper about them."

"Ah," says Albert. "Okay, now it's nearly 5:30 when this next chap turns up." They watch as a man turns toward the church and then disappears from sight down the walkway. "Know him?"

"George Harpole," Charles says, "medievalist from Hull.

I don't really know him, but he was attending the Grail Conference."

They continue watching. Harpole re-appears on the screen after leaving the church, and the time display indicates that it's 6:10. Harpole turns down the High Street in the direction of the hotel.

"So he's been inside the church for a little over half an hour," Edwin points out. "No sign of the boy."

"Not until it's pushing 7 o'clock," Albert says. Appearing on the screen now is a shot of Peter. He's moving hurriedly and passes quickly through the picture.

"Seems in a bit of a rush," Albert says.

"He had a bus to catch," Allie says.

"And he missed it," Charles adds.

"Which, I'm guessing, explains how you two got hooked up with the lad?" Edwin says.

"I'd met him briefly on Thursday afternoon up on the Tor," Charles says, "so it wasn't entirely a matter of 'the kindness of strangers.' We weren't total strangers."

"And Peter doesn't look a bit like Blanche Dubois," Albert says. His remark brings a baffled look from Edwin.

"We took Peter to dinner and brought him back to the hotel afterward," Allie says. "Then on Sunday morning we ran him back to his school."

" 'I was a stranger and you took me in, I was hungry and you fed me,' " Edwin says.

"I don't think you're quoting Tennessee Williams," Albert says.

"Peter's a special lad," Allie says. "We were happy to take him in and feed him."

Albert pauses the tape for moment while they each help themselves to more items from Mrs. Hawkins' tea tray.

"I can't remember the last time I've had a Jaffa Cake," Albert says, biting into one of them. "Honestly, it's not half bad. I've long been accustomed to Edwin's lowbrow tastes, but Allie, I never would have suspected it of you."

"It's all Charlie's fault. His pretense of having working-class values seems to have rubbed off on me."

"Ouch," says Charlie.

"Anyway," Albert says, getting back to business, "we'll need to find the boy and interview him, even though we think it's unlikely he had anything to do with later events."

"We can tell you where he goes to school," Allie says. "But please, try not to cause him any embarrassment among his school fellows. Boys his age are sensitive to things like that."

"After the boy leaves," Albert goes on, "there's nothing significant on the tape for a good while, not until about 10:20. That's when these two chaps appear." Entering the picture now are two men neither Charles nor Allie recognizes. One tallish and slender, the other one burlier.

"Don't know the blokes," Allie says. "Never seen 'em before."

"Me, neither," Charles says.

"Albert and I noticed the thick-set fellow in the hotel lobby," Edwin says. "He passed through twice. Not a hotel guest, so not sure what he was up to."

Then the screen shows another man, this time one Charles does recognize. "That's Geoff Rawlinson," he says. "He's another medievalist from Hull, George Harpole's colleague."

"And a man soon to be deceased," Albert says.

"Oh!" Allie cries out. "It's his body we saw in the chapel!"

"Indeed it is," Albert replies. "Now watch."

The pair of unidentified men appear on the screen after leaving the church. It's obvious they're in a hurry. Together they head up the High Street striding quickly out of the picture.

"Now, what do you suppose those fellows were up to inside the church, eh?" Edwin asks.

"Nothing good," Albert remarks. "It's imperative that we identify them."

"Don't know 'em," Charles says again.

"And now, here at last, we have the three amigos," Albert says. Nigel Bright-Rogers, Sorley MacPherson, and Martin Nicholson come into the picture. It's nearly 11:15. Four minutes later according to the time display, although it seems almost immediate, the threesome re-appears on the screen, their movements suggesting they're in a panic. They separate quickly, each one hurrying off alone, Nicholson haring up the High Street, MacPherson heading back toward the hotel, and Bright-Rogers crossing the street coming straight toward the camera mounted above the shop.

"And now for the stars of the show," Edwin says with a smile in his voice, as Allie, Charles, and the professor appear on the screen. It's a little before midnight. A moment later Eva joins them. The four of them stand there in conversation, then move toward the church and disappear from sight.

And then, it's Edwin who appears on screen. "Boo, hiss," says Albert, "who let this guy in?" Edwin, too, disappears from the screen. Then the screen goes blank and Albert removes the thumb drive. "That's all folks," he says.

"So," Edwin says," what do you make of all of these doings?"

Charles and Allie sit there quietly for a long moment. Finally, Charles speaks up. "Looks to me like you have a clear *terminus ab quo* and *terminus ad quem*. That is, in regard to Rawlinson's death."

"Explain yourself," Albert says.

"The monitor showed that he was alive at 10:20, and we know that he was not alive when we went into the church just going on midnight."

"So, it's probable," Allie adds, "that the two unknown men did the deed, or else Bright-Rogers and his pals did it. They were the only ones in the church between the *quo* and the *quem*."

"What's this *quo* and *quem* business?" Edwin asks.

"You should ask my father," Allie says. "He taught me that before he taught me to how to play darts or cribbage."

"Means 'the end from which' and 'the end to which'," Charles adds. Scholars use them to date works or manuscripts or things like that, based on various bits of external and internal evidence."

"Give me an example," Edwin says.

"Okay. Shakespeare's sonnets were first published in 1609 (that would be the *ad quem*), but there's an earlier reference to them in a work that dates to 1598. So, by then he must've been working on them—so 1598 is the *ab quo*."

"Okay, if you say so," Edwin replies.

"The evidence," Albert says, "shows that one or the other of these two sets of men must've killed Rawlinson. We know you didn't do it, thanks to Edwin arriving on the scene right on your heels—not that we would have suspected you in any case—and we strongly lean toward it being the two unknown men."

"You don't need to be Sherlock Holmes to come to that conclusion," Edwin says.

"You don't even need to be Katie Holmes," Allie says.

"Uh, no," Albert says, looking slightly nonplused, "probably not."

"So," Edwin says, "we're doing everything possible to identify and find these men."

"But a lot of other questions need answering," Albert says.

"Like, what was Geoff Rawlinson doing at the church?" Charles says. "And why was he killed? And what were Bright-Rogers and his pals doing going to the church at that hour of the night? Not just going to see the replicas like we were; they were the ones who'd had the replicas made in the first place. Oh, and like why did George Harpole go to the church earlier in the evening?"

"Yes, quite. That's several of the most crucial ones, my friend," Albert says. "Any follow-up suggestions?"

"I'd want to grill Martin Nicholson," Allie says, "get him to explain what the three of them were up to at the church.

Nicholson's probably an easier nut to crack than either Bright-Rogers or MacPherson."

"Exactly what we thought," says Edwin. "In fact, we've already done that."

"Great minds thinking in parallel," Charles says.

"And *did* he crack?" Allie asks.

"Yes, after a little gentle persuasion. He claims they went to the church to buy an ancient artifact from Rawlinson and Harpole. He says he doesn't know what the artifact was or what has happened to it. Thinks that whoever killed Rawlinson must've taken it. Neither Bright-Rogers nor Sorely MacPherson confirm his story—they both claim to know nothing about any ancient artifact—but we tend to believe his story. What do you think?"

Allie looks at Charles as if to say, "The ball's in your court. Tell them about the artifact, or don't. It's your call."

"Goodness," Charles says, trying to think fast. His initial conclusion is that it's better for the artifact to be in the professional hands of men like Oldhouse and his friend at the Pitt-Rivers than in the hands of government officials. So, as much as he likes Albert and Edwin, that's what guides his words.

"I don't know what to say, other than that you must find those men."

"So, you know nothing of any artifact?" Edwin asks.

Charles shrugs. "I know that Allie and I have no ancient artifacts—not unless that cricket bat on the mantelpiece qualifies."

"I noticed it," Albert admits. "I surely hope you don't plan to play cricket with it."

On their way out, Edwin and Albert stop to thank Mrs. Hawkins for her lovely tea. Then they saunter on down the driveway to the street.

"I really do like that young couple," Albert says.

"I do as well," Edwin agrees, "even if they aren't telling us everything they know."

"But they will, eventually."

"Oh, yes, they certainly will—eventually."

❖

On Thursday evening, Charles and Allie have a quiet meal in Charles' flat, then take a long, leisurely walk out to the Trout Pub in Wolvercote.

"Charles," Allie says as they stroll along, "I don't suppose you're familiar with Shaftesbury."

"That would be correct. I've heard of Shaftesbury, and I have a vague sense of where it is, but that's about it. Why?"

"What do you mean 'Why?' Don't you know?"

"Umm, no, 'fraid not."

"Peter's game. It's where Peter's soccer game is tomorrow afternoon. Why don't we go? Give us a chance to see him again and to put this ghastly business out of our minds for a few hours."

"Allie," Charles says, "every now and then you come up with a brilliant idea."

"Well . . . you needn't sound so surprised."

CHAPTER 17
— A Perfect Day —

Charles and Allie are ten miles out of Oxford on Friday morning when Charles says, "Think we could stop for an hour or two in Salisbury on our way to Shaftesbury? I was glancing at the map and it's hardly out of our way."

"Every now and then you come up with a brilliant idea," Allie replies.

Allie's verbal jab makes Charles smile.

"Salisbury Cathedral," she says. "It's my second favorite of all the great English cathedrals, just the tiniest bit behind Wells."

It's another bright April morning. They tool along in Allie's little roadster with the top down, Allie handling the wheel like she thinks she's Stirling Moss, and it isn't long before they're heading south on the A303. Charles smiles, reflecting on the fact that a person's driving style can reveal a lot about their personality.

"What have you heard from the chap at the Pitt-Rivers?" she asks.

"He wants me and the professor to come by on Monday afternoon. Thinks he may have some answers by then."

"What did you think of him?"

"Not so stuffy as I'd feared he might be. Quite an engaging fellow, actually."

"My father would be disappointed. He thinks there's just one man in Oxford who isn't stuffy."

"Not two of us?"

"You don't count, Charlie, you aren't English. No, only the professor."

"Who was rescued from stuffiness by spending a year at Berkeley in the late '60s."

"That could well be true, though Dad says he wasn't stuffy even when he was an undergraduate at Oxford, in spite of being the smartest kid on the block."

"That expression sounds like an Americanism."

"I've been working on them, Charlie, just in case I may need them sometime." They exchange sly glances, a hint of a smile on each of their lips.

When the top of the spire of Salisbury Cathedral suddenly appears poking up above the hills surrounding the small, low-lying city, Charles says, "Oh, my word!"

"A British-ism, Charlie? Yes, it's splendid—tallest spire in Britain. I've read that in all of Europe, only the one at Cologne Cathedral is higher, and then, just by a few feet."

They spend two hours in Salisbury rather than one—touring the cathedral and admiring its many splendors. Charles finds the frieze of biblical scenes, both Old Testament and New, that adorn the walls of the chapter house, especially captivating. He and Ally pause to study the scene of the crucifixion, looking for the lance of Longinus. It's not there. One thing that is there, nearby, is a copy of the Magna Carta. Charles spends a few minutes examining it. "I had no idea that was here," he says to her.

"There's another copy in Lincoln Cathedral," she says, "and a third one somewhere, I think in London, maybe the British Museum or British Library."

Before hitting the road again they lunch at a charming little pub—The Checkers—Allie knows about just across the water meadows from the town. There's a good view of the cathedral from there, too, and Charles is glad he's brought his camera.

"Constable painted the cathedral from a vantage point somewhere around here," Allie says.

"I'll pass on the Constable," Charles says. "No, what I really want is an original Alwyn Tremayne painting of the cathedral. Could I talk you into doing one for me?"

"Well . . . I'll think about it," she says, coyly. "What would it be worth to you?"

"More than silver and gold," he says.

"More than that? Well, I'll think about it. But you could throw in a little silver and gold, too, just for good measure."

Shaftesbury being a small town, it's no problem to spot the school complex where Peter's soccer game will be played. But it's only a little after 2:30 when they arrive in Shaftesbury and the game isn't until four, so they have plenty of time to wander about the quaint little town before heading to the game. The town itself is perched on the edge of an intriguing area of southwest Britain known as the Cranborne Chase, an area famous for its natural beauty and many ancient remains. "It's called a 'chase'," Allie tells Charles, "because in early times, members of the noble class, often including the royals, came here to hunt, to chase after the deer."

They enter the school grounds a bit before four and follow other folks who are making their way to the football pitch. Allie and Charles take seats about halfway up the little grandstand, then watch as the lads on the field stretch and run warm-up drills. Peter's side is kitted out in purple jerseys with white pinstripes and white shorts; the home side wears white jerseys with red lettering, red shorts and red knee socks. The boys' movements on the emerald-green field create an ever-shifting kaleidoscope of color.

Most of the fans in the grandstand are obviously supporting the home side, but there's a small clutch who are cheering for Peter's team. Charles looks them over, trying to guess which ones are parents and which ones might be teachers or staff members who've come up from Peter's school. There's a few he's not at all sure of.

From the outset, the home side dominates the game, having numerous shots on goal, one of which finally goes in. But as the first half continues, Peter's side begins to play with increasing confidence, and the game tightens up. They are down 2-nil when a boy named Dickie breaks away and sends the ball rocketing into the left corner of the net. Then, less than a minute later, Peter lofts a long, looping kick that just eludes the goalie's reach. Now the game is tied up and the visiting fans cheer lustily.

Charles notices a young woman and a young man seated a few rows below them. Throughout the game she's been shouting her encouragement for Peter, and she's ecstatic when he scores. "Huzzah! Score one for Tottenham." Charles, even from a distance, can make out the boy's grin.

When Allie adds her voice to the cheers for Peter, the young woman turns and glances back to see who this additional female fan might be.

The score remains tied at the interval. Many of the fans get to their feet and begin moving about. One of the men Charles has pegged as being a parent slides over and asks Charles if he and Allie might be Peter's relatives. "You know the lad, I take it," he says, "but you surely aren't his parents."

"No, not his parents," Charles replies, "just friends who happened to be in the area."

"Well, you couldn't have picked a better day for a game," the man adds, smiling. "I'm Richard Davis, Dickie's father. My son and Peter are close friends. Isn't it grand that each of them has scored a goal? And maybe the lads will come through today. They aren't expected to win this one, but, you never know."

In the second half the game goes back and forth. The home sides scores to take the lead again, but then Dickie scores a second goal to pull his side even. As the final seconds of regular time wind down, Dickie lifts a corner kick high in front of the goal, and Peter knifes in under it, tilts his neck, and heads the ball through the upraised hands of the goalkeeper.

"Score!" shouts the young woman in front of them.

"Huzzah!" shouts Allie. The home fans emit a collective

groan. Time expires and the home team has lost, 4-3.

The homeside fans go down and commiserate with the dispirited boys. Peter's team's lesser number of fans congregate behind the bench, offering their warm congratulations. "Great header, Peter! Well, done, Dickie! What a perfect corner kick!"

"Oh, sir!" Peter cries when he spots Charles, "you came to the game! Oh, miss, you're here too. How wonderful to see you."

"You were brilliant, Peter," Allie says. "Move over, Harry Kane, make way for Peter Saunders!"

The young woman Charles has been watching comes over and hugs Peter. "My brother, the superstar," she says cheerily. The young man with her stands shyly by.

"Hi, Gordon," Peter says. "Really glad you could come. I guess Sheila must've commandeered you, hmm?"

"A most enjoyable game, Peter," the young man says. "You were great."

"Sheila," Peter says, "these are my friends from Oxford. Sheila's my sister," he says to Charles and Allie. "She and Gordon drove up from Exeter."

Peter's coach gathers the boys for his post-game remarks. Then they all begin to move toward the team van, Charles walking alongside Peter. When they are out of earshot of the others Peter says, "Sir, I saw some news articles about a man who was killed in Glastonbury last week. Have you seen them?"

"Yes, I have. Pretty creepy stuff."

"They found his body in the church, right near where the

holy lances were on display."

"That's my understanding."

"Goodness. And I'd been in there just a few hours before, too."

"I don't know what it was all about, Peter, but I doubt if anyone would have meant you any harm."

"I've been wondering, sir, about that object we found—that lance head or whatever it was. Do you still have it?"

"A scientist in Oxford has it at the moment. He's trying to form some conclusions about it. We should know more in just a few days."

"That's splendid, sir. Oh, and my mum says it's fine for me to visit you in Oxford. She said she thinks it's a marvelous idea. Her words exactly."

"That's terrific, Peter. Do you think next weekend might be a possibility? That is, if you don't already have other plans?'

"We have a home match on Thursday afternoon, but after that, I have nothing until the next week."

"Then why don't we come to your match, and we can all drive back to Oxford afterward. Then we'll run you back to school on Sunday afternoon."

"Oh, sir, that sounds splendid."

"Peter, about that man who was killed in Glastonbury. The police have already talked to us about it. They'll probably want to talk to you, too. We had nothing useful to tell them."

"Goodness. Well, I'll tell them what I did, that I went into the church to see the lances. Do you think I should say anything about what I did with the lancehead?"

Charles notices the boy nervously twisting his toe in the turf. "No," Charles says, "I don't see any need for you to do that. Not unless they bring it up."

"Good, because I still feel a little embarrassed about what I did, moving the thing and all."

"I doubt if that had anything to do with anything, Peter," Charles says, though he's not at all sure that's true.

"Good. That's a bit of a relief."

Charles and Allie are driving north toward Oxford in the Vale of the White Horse when Charles suddenly says, "Why don't we pull off onto that little country lane up there and give ourselves a brief respite from the drive."

"You think we should?'

"I do. I definitely do. We're in no hurry."

"Then why don't we just do that."

It's a quiet little lane with rolling green pastureland and a sprinkling of cows on each side. They mosey along for half a mile in rural solitude. Then Charles says, "There's nothing like the beauteous splendor of the English countryside in April. Hey, why don't you see if you can't just snug your car in behind that huge oak tree up there."

"I'll give it a try. Might just be able to."

After Allie maneuvers her car behind the tree and switches off the engine, Charles reaches toward her, puts his arm about her shoulders, and pulls her to him.

"Ah ha, now I see what you're up to," she says.

"You think I'm up to no good?"

"I wouldn't put it that way."

Charles looks deeply into Allie's light blue eyes. She presses her face against Charles' neck, then tilts her face upward in invitation, offering her lips.

"I'd say this is a perfect way to end a perfect day," he says.

"Oh, Charlie, it is . . . oh my, . . . it is.

CHAPTER 18
— Time's Wingèd Chariot —

George Harpole stares down at the black water several hundred feet below. It's cold standing there on the Humber River Bridge, wind gusts buffeting him. He knows the statistics—that only five of the more than 200 people who have either jumped or fallen from the bridge have survived. But . . . surviving isn't his intention.

"Oh, Nadja," he whispers. "If only we'd had world enough and time."

Then more words from the famous poem appear in his head: *'Thou by the Indian Ganges' side . . . I by the tide of Humber . . . but at my back I sometimes hear . . .'*

What George suddenly hears at his back isn't 'Time's wingèd chariot' but a huge lorry barreling across the long bridge. The driver gives him a blast of its horn, and the lorry doesn't slow down at all.

"Go ahead, George," says a voice. It's Geoff. "Come join us. We're waiting for you."

"No, George, no," comes a second voice. It's Nadja. "It wasn't you. It was us. We made our choices. You were our friend. You didn't fail us, we failed you."

"Jump, George," Geoff says. "For once in your useless life,

prove that you aren't a coward. Screw your courage to the sticking place, George. *Jump!*"

"No, George, no."

George feels like Dr. Faustus listening to a debate between his Good Angel and his Bad Angel. He tries to remember which of them got the last word.

Then George hears another voice, not in his head but coming from behind him. "I'm sorry, sir," says the voice, "but you need to return to your car. It's hazardous for you to be stopping here on the bridge like this. Didn't you see the 'No Stopping on Bridge' signs?"

Lost in his thoughts, George hadn't been aware of the police car that had pulled up behind his own car a moment ago. "Oh, yes, right," George says, his muzzy brain finally returning to the here and now. "Yes, yes, I'll just do that."

George climbs back into his car and the policeman into his. The man follows George until George has reached the far side of the bridge, then the police car wheels about and heads back across the bridge.

❖

It's nearing ten on Saturday morning as Eva leaves her basement flat in Norham Gardens. A man who's been sitting on a bench reading a newspaper rises to his feet and trails slowly along behind her. Eva turns left onto the Banbury Road, strolling toward central Oxford. It seems pretty obvious to the man behind her that she intends to be out for a good while, so he pulls out his cell phone and calls his confederate. The coast is clear, he informs him. He should have plenty of time to make a thorough search of the woman's little flat.

Clocks are sounding the hour of ten as Eva moves quickly along St. Giles Street and into Cornmarket Street. She's meeting Dennis Adams for coffee at ten and doesn't want to keep him waiting. Truth be told, she's eager to see him. She likes the fact that he's been pursuing her so avidly. It's given her ego a nice little boost.

Eva doesn't notice the slendor fellow with the prominent nose who's been shadowing her movements ever since she left her little basement flat. And when she enters the Cup & Chaucer coffee shop, she doesn't notice that he does too, only seconds behind her.

Eva sees Dennis already seated at a table. He rises halfway from his chair and lifts a hand when he sees her come in. Dennis, captivated by the sight of Eva, also fails to notice the man who takes a seat at a little table close behind them.

Eva and Dennis smile at each other. "'Morning, sir," she says, reaching out a hand. Dennis wears a dark brown sweater which nearly matches his dark brown owl-eyes.

"'Morning, miss," he replies, taking her hand and giving it a little squeeze. Eva can't help looking at Dennis's head, trying to spot the place behind his ear where he'd sustained the serious blow the previous weekend.

"Yes," he says, seeing where her eyes have gone, "there's still a good-sized bump there, but I've figured out how to comb over it." His owl-eyes shine behind his round glasses.

After the waitress has filled coffee cups and taken their order, Eva asks, "So, how are you feeling, Dennis?"

"Surprisingly good. My bosses have insisted on putting me

on leave, but it wasn't really necessary they do that. Gives me a good chance, though, to come and visit Oxford. To come and visit you, Eva."

"I suppose I shouldn't ask, but I can't help wondering. Dennis, do you have any idea who attacked you and why? Any notions about that at all?"

"Not really. It must've been someone who'd realized what I was doing in Glastonbury and concluded that I posed some sort of a threat to them."

"So, you were in Glastonbury on a job?"

"Oh yes, I was. But then I saw you, Eva, and the pursuit of my personal pleasure rubbed up against fulfilling my responsibilities." Dennis adds cream and sugar to his coffee and gives it a good stir, then takes a sip.

"You don't think they meant to kill you, do you?"

"No, probably not. If they had, they would have succeeded. It's quite certain that the men who did those things in Glastonbury were pros."

"So that fellow inside the church, the man they did kill . . ."

"They *meant* to kill. For god knows what reason."

"You think the two attacks are related?"

"Almost certainly."

"And what about the death of the woman in Hull? That's related as well?"

"That's the probability."

"More coffee sir?" says a young woman holding a shining urn.

"Yes, please."

"And you?" she says to Eva.

"Just a drop, thank you."

"Oh, and could you bring us a couple of Danishes?" Dennis asks.

When the waitress is gone Eva says, "That was a horrifying scene my friends and I stumbled upon that night inside the church. I'll be having bad dreams about that for the rest of my life. Have you any idea what that was all about?"

"Yes and no. It's likely that it was related to the matter I was looking into. Why it took that particular turn, I've no idea."

"A woman murdered in Hull. A man killed in Glastonbury, and another man attacked and knocked out in Glastonbury. Goodness. And the two people who were murdered weren't just murdered—they were *crucified*. Dennis, this isn't child's play, is it? I have to say, I'm so glad that you are free and clear of it, at least for now."

"And maybe for good. Since it involves homicide, the big boys have taken over and some of us smaller fry been shunted off to the side. Only a subordinate role for use henceforth."

"I want you to be safe," she says, "that's the important thing." Dennis reaches out and places his hand atop hers. His gentle touch feels wonderful to her.

"I'll be fine," he says. "Don't you worry about me."

"I do worry about you," she replies.

Through the door of the coffee shop strides a familiar figure. Eva looks up and says loudly, "Professor! Come over and join us."

"Just for a moment," Professor Wentworth replies, "just

until they have my coffee ready. Then it's back to the salt mines."

"Salt mines? You're hard at it on a Saturday morning, Professor?"

"It's my favorite time. Very quiet in college on Saturday morning. My wife's gone off to the Costa del Sol with her gal-pals for a week in the sun, and I'm all on my own for a few days. A free man, so to speak."

"So, it's the siren call of your musty old manuscripts?"

"Quite right, my dear. And I have just encountered something quite good that will definitely be of interest to Charlie, too."

"Something involving Chaucer?"

"Of course something involving Chaucer."

"Not Malory?"

"Eva," the professor says, tilting his head and staring down at her over his glasses.

"Dennis," Eva says, "what's that adage about old dogs and new tricks?"

"This old dog," the professor says, "does *no* tricks, old or new. This old dog is a Chaucer scholar, pure and simple."

"Not so pure and not so simple," Eva says, "but very damn good at being a Chaucer scholar."

"Well, thank you, my dear, I *think* that might have been meant to be a compliment. Anyway, I'd best get back to my rooms in college. Nice to just hole up there for a few days and work and not have to wander back home of an evening."

"It's nice to see you sir," Dennis says. "Give my regards to

Chaucer." Witty repartee isn't one of Dennis's strong points. Eva finds that refreshing in a town she believes places too high a premium on wit.

The professor looks over his glasses at Dennis but doesn't say anything. Then he steps over to the counter and collects the large coffee that's there awaiting him. With coffee in hand, he heads for the coffee shop door.

Striding a few steps behind Professor Wentworth is the man who'd been eavesdropping on Eva and Dennis. After what he's gleaned from the conversation he just overheard, he's decided to shift his focus from the young woman and onto the elderly professor.

Albert and Edwin step out through the door of the pasty shop on Cornmarket Street. They hold carrier bags containing their fresh, hot pasties and orders of chips.

"Don't look now," Albert says, "but here comes the old professor already. He didn't spend much time in the coffee shop, did he?"

"Got his coffee and scones to take-away, apparently."

The two men watch as the professor walks toward the corner of Queen Street and High Street, then turns left onto the High.

"Wait," cautions Edwin. He puts his hand on Albert's arm. "What have we here?" Trailing along behind the professor they see a tall, slim man.

"Now that chap could well be someone we're interested in, couldn't he?"

"Indeed, he could. Altered his appearance a bit but still quite recognizable. Hard to hide that distinctive nose of his."

As they watch, it's apparent that the man is following the professor. He remains half a block behind the professor as the pair of them move down High Street, Albert and Edwin moseying along behind them. They walk past the Covered Market on their left and then St. Mary's Church, with its towering spire. When the professor crosses the street and heads off to the right toward his college, the man who's been pursuing him stops and stands behind on High Street.

"I'll stick with the professor," Albert says. "You stay with our unknown friend."

They watch as the man pulls out his cell phone and makes a call. They can't hear him, but what he says is, "The professor's going to be staying in his office at the college, so I'm off to Headington to check out his home. That will leave us just the American's flat in Summertown. That one will be tougher because of the landlady and her dog, but we'll find a way."

He shuts his phone, looks up, and realizes that he's standing close to a stop for a bus that will take him the short distance to Headington. As a bus pulls up, he hops on and the bus zips off on its way. Edwin, fifty yards away, watches helplessly as the bus moves on down the High Street.

"Bloody hell!" Edwin says. He knows he's just made a rookie mistake, lost his prey with no readily available transport, since they've left their car in a public lot several blocks away. He looks for a taxi but of course there's none in sight—hard to find them in Oxford unless you're at the train station.

"Bloody hell!" he says again. He watches the big red bus disappearing down the High Street. moving toward Magdalen Bridge.

❖

"I bought you a present," Allie says. "Got it yesterday when we were poking about in Shaftesbury. It's a bit scuffed up, I'm afraid, but I know how you prefer old things to new ones." She and Charles are sitting in Mrs. Hawkins' garden drinking coffee and eating hot buttered scones with jam, enjoying a lazy Saturday morning.

"A present? For me? No one ever gives me presents."

Allie reaches her hand into her bag but doesn't pull anything out. "You have to guess what it is."

"Give me a clue?"

"It's manly but pleasurable."

"Woo, sounds kind of erotic."

"No, wrong."

"Maybe a basketball? Or a John D. MacDonald Travis McGee novel? Or a medieval manuscript containing an unknown poem possibly by Geoffrey Chaucer?"

"All wrong. Basketball was close-ish, though." Allie reaches into her bag and pulls out a small leather spheroid. She tosses it to Charles who snags it with his right hand.

"That's a very small basketball," he says.

"It's a cricket ball, goof-head. As if you didn't know. What good is a cricket bat without a cricket ball?" Charles grips the small ball. It's about the size and weight of a baseball, he thinks, though the external leather sections are arranged completely differently.

Allie's cell phone suddenly jingles inside her bag. She fishes it out, then stares at the screen a moment with a scrunched-up face before saying, "Hello?"

"It's for you, Charlie," she says, handing it to him, the look on her face almost as surprised as his.

"Hello," he says, then listens a moment to a smooth, plummy voice he recognizes as that of Nigel Bright-Rogers. "Excuse me," Charles says, "but how did you get this number? From Allie's father, perhaps?" He shoots Allie a questioning look. "Ah, from her web site."

"Yes," Bright-Rogers say, "your friend is quite an accomplished artist, you know."

"I do know."

"Sir, we believe you have in your possession an object that we would like very much like to purchase from you."

"No idea what you're talking about. What gives you that idea?"

"The information comes from your good friend Professor Wentworth. He's told my old colleague, Oliver-John Oldhouse at the Ashmolean, about it. So, we're confident the information is correct."

"Well, then, what is it you're proposing?"

"This object—or rather artifact or relic—properly belongs in a museum. It would be a huge feather in our cap if we could add it to our collection in Manchester. Not quite like the British Museum having the Rosetta Stone, perhaps, but a bit along those lines, eh? We'd like to purchase it from you, and we're willing to remunerate you handsomely. Also, we'll credit you with the find. Does that sound good?"

"It does. Unfortunately, the professor's information was incorrect. We don't have any artifact. But if it should turn up, we could let you know."

"Oh, well, I think you are toying with me. Let me assure you that it's worth 450,000 euros to us. Surely you can find a use for such a sum. That's probably the equivalent of six or eight years of salary for you in the U.S."

"That's certainly an intriguing offer. Anyway, we'll keep you posted."

"Yes, do bear it in mind. And do make up your mind about our offer—sooner rather than later."

"Nice chatting with you."

"And with you."

Charles hands Allie her phone. "Bright-Rogers has offered us 450,000 euros for the spear-head."

"Cheap bastard," Allie says, and they both laugh.

"Someone seems to have let the cat out of the bag—either Oldhouse or Jonathan Owens, the chap at the Pitt-Rivers."

"Or maybe the professor?"

"Yes, I suppose that is a possibility."

"Or, maybe Bright-Rogers was just taking a stab in the dark, hoping that we might be the ones who have it."

"Yes, that's a possibility, too."

❖

Eva and Dennis are still in the coffee shop when the clocks chime eleven. They're still there when the clocks chime twelve. "Goodness," Eva says, "noon already."

"I'm in no particular hurry," Dennis says.

"Nor am I," she replies. Eva wonders if she should be so bold as to invite Dennis back to her flat. She's never invited a man there before. The thought excites her. But no, she thinks, he might think that's rather forward of me. No need to be rushing things. For now, steady as she goes. She certainly doesn't want him thinking she's a round-heeled woman.

Dennis thinks about inviting Eva back to his hotel room in the Randolph Hotel. It's an exciting idea, but no, he decides. Eva might think he's being overly presumptuous. He doesn't want that.

"Want to go punting?" she asks. "We could pack a picnic and make an afternoon of it."

"You'll have to teach me how. Never done it before."

"Oh, you'll pick it up in no time."

"Always willing to try and learn new things," he says.

"Let's go, then, shall we?"

❖

"The fella with the pointy nose," Albert says, "ya let 'im slip through your fingers?"

"He just hopped on the bus, Gus, and got 'imself free, as the man says in the song."

"Slippery bugger, eh? Well, we'll find 'im. Those other two 've gone off ta have themselves a picnic. But as for them, I think we can safely rule 'em out of the picture."

"Yes. But not our cribbage-playing friends."

"Oh, no, not them. If I were a betting man . . ."

"Which you aren't."

"Me? Oh, no, never. But if I were, I'd be good for a tenner

on them being smack in the middle of this business."

"But not the murders."

"No . . . though they may know more about 'em than they're letting on."

"Not at all sure about the old professor. He's a cagey one, bit of a dark horse, the fellow is. Seems to be a dry-as-dust scholar, but there's more to that old gentleman than meets the eye."

"He's a bit of dark horse all right," says Edwin.

"Tomorrow," Albert says, "I think we should split up. I'll keep tabs on the young American and his Cornish companion. You scour the city for our sharp-nosed friend."

"Bert, I do believe you're rather taken by that Cornish lass."

"Yes, well, and your point is, Kemosabe?'

CHAPTER 19
— Information, Disinformation —

During the following week, Peter's thoughts return again and again to his conversation with the police.

The pair of detectives who arrived at the school on Monday afternoon weren't at all like the kind of detectives Peter had seen so often on TV crime shows. With their smiles and soft-spoken manner, they'd seemed entirely benign and gentle. The lead one was a chubby, cheerful, round-faced man; his taller, leaner, quieter companion actually reminded Peter of his Presbyterian minister back home in London.

The men assured Peter he was in no trouble. All they wanted, they said, was to ask him a few questions about his excursion to Glastonbury the previous weekend. They hoped he might be able to help them with their enquiries.

"So Peter, why don't you begin by telling us how you spent your day last Saturday," the round-faced detective had said. "Just run through it from start to finish, telling us everything you did." Peter regaled them with as full an account as he could provide. They listened with apparent interest, but it became clear what they wanted to know about particularly was why he'd gone into the church and what he'd done in there.

"The sign said the church was closed but you went in anyway, Peter," the lead detective said. "Why was that?"

"I just went into the church, sir, because of the exhibition of the lances. It was my only chance to see them. I really needed to do that for the school paper I'm working on. I didn't see how anyone could mind if I slipped in quietly, took a few notes, and then left, leaving everything just as I found it." Peter showed them his notebook with all the information he'd collected about the lances and the sketches he'd drawn of them.

The men seemed satisfied with his explanation. Then they'd asked him about how he'd come to know the acclaimed Oxford professor, his young American friend, and their female companion. They wanted to know what he thought of them.

"Oh, the professor's certainly a brilliant man, sir. I learned a lot about the Middle Ages from him. And the American's quite a learned fellow, too. He knew things up on the Tor that my teacher didn't even know." Then Peter smiled. "He has a sense of humor, too, and he likes teasing the professor. It's obvious that he and the professor are quite fond of each other."

"And the young woman?"

"Miss Tremayne? Oh, sir, I think she's smashing—er, I mean, I quite like her. She was terribly kind to me. It was her idea for her and Mr. Bascombe to bring me all the way back to school on Sunday after I'd missed the last bus on Saturday night. She and Mr. Bascombe even treated me to lunch on Sunday—that makes two meals I owe them."

"When you were inside the church, Peter," the taller one asked, finally joining the conversation, "did anyone else happen to come in while you were there? Did you happen to see anyone else at all doing anything inside the church?'"

Peter thought about the person he'd hidden from, the man who'd left the spearhead hidden behind the display case. Peter hadn't actually seen the man. Should he say anything about that?

Finally, after a long pause, Peter said, "No, I didn't notice anyone one else while I was in the church. If anyone else was about, I certainly didn't see them."

"Well, thank you, Peter," the round-faced one said. "Is there anyone else you met in Glastonbury you want to tell us about?"

"No, I can't think of anyone. Oh, wait a second. Yes, Dr. Xander. I did meet him. He's a London physician. You may have heard of him. He's the one who helped the fellow who'd had the accident in the hotel."

"Any idea, Peter, why the good doctor was in Glastonbury?"

"I think he was there for the conference on the Holy Grail, just like the others. Mr. Bascombe said he was a private scholar."

"Well, Peter, that about wraps things up, I believe. You've been very helpful, son."

Each of the detectives shook hands with the boy, then they departed.

Peter was relieved. He hadn't actually *seen* anyone else in the church, so what he'd said hadn't been an out-and-out falsehood. He'd answered all their questions truthfully—even if he hadn't quite told them everything.

❖

On that same Monday afternoon when Peter is being interviewed by the detectives, Charles and Allie stroll through the University Parks. It's one-thirty, half an hour before Charles has his meeting at the Pitt-Rivers Museum with Jonathan Owens, whose experts have been running tests on the spearhead. Allie has brought along her sketch pad and a paperback novel to occupy her while Charles sees the noted scholar at the museum. She's as excited as he is about what he may soon learn.

"You could come along with me, you know," he says. "That mysterious little object that I hope he will have identified is more yours than mine."

"No, Charlie, it's not either of ours. And besides, you're the academic, not me. It's a lot more in your bailiwick than mine. I'm just some little-known Cornish painter, not some famous Chaucer scholar."

"*Just*? You're *just* some little-known painter? Allie, a note of false humility?"

"False humility, ha, that's also something that's more up your street than mine," she replies tartly. "The pot calling the kettle black?" Charles laughs and shrugs his shoulders in partial agreement.

"Might be a little true of the both of us," he admits.

"Might be truer of one of us than the other," she replies.

"Okay, whatever. You be good, and I'll see you in a bit."

"I'll be on tenterhooks until you return—whatever tenterhooks are."

"Ancient Roman artifacts with sharp metal points," Charles

says.

"Yes, I'm sure, oh learned scholar."

After Charles has left for his meeting, Allie remains seated on a shaded park bench, her sketch pad on her lap. Before long she starts in on a charcoal drawing of Keble College, only a couple of hundred yards away from where she sits. She can't help smiling as she remembers her father's harsh comments about Keble, probably the Oxford college he despised more than any other. When it came to Keble, he never minced words about "that atrocious 19th-century pile of shite with its holy zebra brickwork." Allie doesn't entirely agree with him, but she knows it wouldn't a good idea for her to send him the sketch she's making, though she really does want to send him something. Maybe a drawing of the tower at Magdalen College? Maybe a drawing with the Magdalen Tower looming up behind Magdalen Bridge? That would be a bit of a cliché—done a thousand times before—but he would like it anyway, since it would be a work by his beloved daughter depicting one of the few bits of Oxford architecture that he actually does admire.

When Charles enters Jonathan Owens' office in the Pitt-Rivers Museum, he discovers that Professor Wentworth is already there. The two men are enjoying cups of tea and munching on hobnobs.

"Tea, Charles?" Owens asks.

"Coffee would be better, if it's available," Charles replies.

"No problem at all."

"Now then," Owens says a few moments later after his assistant has brought Charles a fresh cup of coffee, "this object you've asked us to have a look at, Mr. Bascombe, proves to be quite a tantalizing artifact. We've studied it and run several tests on it and have some preliminary notions about it. Of course, we can't actually date the metal point, but we have been able to establish an approximate age for the bit of wooden shaft still attached to it. The wood, by the way, is ash and we can date it roughly to a 100-year period—that would be sometime during last century B.C. until perhaps midway through the first century A.D."

Charles and the professor exchange knowing looks.

"You rather expected that?" Jon Owens asks.

"Thought it a good possibility," the professor says, nodding.

"We can't be nearly so precise about the dating of the spearhead. What we can say with some confidence is that it's quite typical of a variety of Roman lance that was known during that period as a *hasta*."

Charles leans forward in his chair, cupping his chin in one hand. This is what he's waited for. The professor, for his part, taps his fingers nervously on his thigh.

"The *hasta*," Owens continues, "was commonly in use during the Republic but then later on, not so much. You are probably less familiar with that variety of lance than you may be with the Roman *pilum*. Unlike the *pilum*, which was a throwing weapon, the *hasta* was used as a thrusting or stabbing weapon. It's barbless, as you can see. The smooth edges allow for a quick stab and then a quick extraction, enabling the warrior to stab his foe again in another spot, or to stab a different enemy."

The professor grins, and Charles takes a sip of coffee to mask his own delight. The man is confirming what they had suspected.

"The *hasta* had a fairly long shaft, usually about two meters in length. The shaft was commonly made of ash, like this one. To put it more into your medieval frame of reference, it was sort of a Roman equivalent to the medieval pike, which I'm sure you chaps are quite familiar with."

"So," the professor says, "you're saying that it's the head of a Roman thrusting spear."

"Undoubtedly, it is."

The professor looks toward Charles with tilted head. Charles, lips compressed, nods several times, the only outward sign of his inward excitement.

"And how rare is such an object?" the professor asks.

"As well-preserved as this one? *Quite* rare."

"Were you able to ascertain if there were any traces of blood on the spearhead?" Charles asks.

"Yes, we could and there were. But so little of it and so degraded, not possible to analyze in any meaningful way."

Again, Charles nods. Then the three men sit in silence for a long moment. Charles takes another big sip from his coffee cup and the professor reaches out for another hobnob.

"So," Jonathon Owens says, "what plans do you have for this most intriguing artifact, now that you know a bit more about it? I have to say that it's quite a valuable object and any museum—including the BM, the V&A, the Ashmolean, or *us*—would be pleased to have it in their collection. Any chance you would be open to parting with it? For a reasonable sum, of course. No offense, gentlemen, but this little treasure really should be in the care of professionals."

"No offense taken," Charles replies.

"It really shouldn't be rattling around in a shoe box on the top shelf of your wardrobe."

"How did you know?" Charles says, grinning.

"Well, please do assure me you will have it under lock and key. And please do keep in mind our offer to buy it. I can't give you a precise number off the top of my head, but it would probably be at least four, maybe even five, figures. A tidy little sum."

"Goodness," Charles says. "Well, that's definitely worth thinking about."

"Of course," Jonathan Owens says with a smile, "you could always just donate it to our museum. I assure you, we should be most grateful."

The three men shake hands, and Charles and the professor depart.

"Should we rendezvous for coffee in the morning and kick this around a bit, now we have the expert opinion?" Charles asks.

"Nine o'clock at Brown's Café?"

"That works for me," Charles says, "see you then."

With the artifact secured inside the small protective case which Jonathan Owens had given to him, Charles heads back to the University Parks to find Allie.

Charles pauses thirty yards from the bench where Allie sits sketching away. The young woman is deeply involved in her work. He watches as she frowns at the page, then makes a small alteration. There's just no getting around it, Charles thinks, Alwyn Tremayne is breath-takingly beautiful.

He stands there and imbibes the sight of her—her round, sculpted cheeks, her widely spaced light blue eyes, her graceful nose and full shapely lips, the honey-hued skin of her neck, her head framed by her honey blond hair. As she scrutinizes her drawing, she unconsciously nibbles on the end of her pencil. Charles can't help smiling.

Allie looks up and sees him standing there smiling at her. She breaks into a smile also, a smile so dazzling that Charles is nearly bowled over. How did I ever get so effin' lucky, he says to himself.

CHAPTER 20
— Unexpected Developments —

Eva Brooksby is ecstatic. She's been offered a job! It's a three-year contract at the University of Leeds, which is quite a good university. Not Oxford, of course, but it could be far, far worse. While she hates the idea of leaving Oxford, Eva has known all along that that was pretty much inevitable.

Eva phones Dennis, who had returned to London on Monday, and she shares her news with him.

"That's wonderful," he says. "Eva, we must celebrate, dinner and a show at the least. Could you possibly come this Friday? I can get us some tickets to whatever West End show you'd like to see. Give it a think, eh?"

"Oh, Dennis, that sounds splendid," she replies.

"Listen, I insist, Eva. You must stay over on Friday night in my flat."

"In your flat?"

"Yes. And, uh, I can camp out on my sofa for a night or two, no problem at all."

"Oh, Dennis, you needn't do that. Not, that is, unless all you have is a single bed."

"No, actually, my bed's a queen."

"Then Dennis, I see no problem at all about my staying over in your flat."

❖

At ten on Tuesday morning, after having coffee in Brown's Café, Charles and Professor Wentworth find themselves seated comfortably in the office of Oliver-John Oldhouse at the Ashmolean Museum. Oliver-John, looking like a dapper old fox, with his russet-colored, gray-tinged hair, his neatly trimmed beard, and his lavender bowtie, leans forward and picks up the small container Charles has placed on his desk.

"So, my friend Jonathan was able to give you a pretty good idea of what we might have here, eh?"

"He certainly did that," the professor says. "Went a long way toward confirming our suspicions." Oldhouse nods and smiles.

"So now," Charles adds, "we have a pretty good notion what the artifact is, and also, what it might *additionally* be."

"As do I," Oldhouse says, "as do I. Just to expedite matters, should you wish to go in that direction, I've already made contact with certain parties in Italy. They say they would most certainly be interested in the artifact, should it prove to be what they hope it might be. I went ahead and took that initiative, sirs, because, to be frank, *they* truly are the ones who should have it."

"A bit presumptuous of you, Oliver-John," says the professor.

"Yes, yes, I admit it. Still, professional ethics required it."

"Well," the professor says, "it's up to Allie and Charles." He looks at Charles.

"Sir," Charles says to Oldhouse, "if it's what we both think it may be, that would make it one of the holiest objects in all of Christendom." Oldhouse nods his agreement. "It should be in a place where it can be properly venerated." Oldhouse nods again, a small smile beginning to creep across his vulpine face. "Sir, if you could facilitate a meeting with the folks you've contacted, if they are the appropriate parties, we would be most grateful."

"Brilliant," Oldhouse says.

The professor reaches over and pats Charles' shoulder. "Well done, lad."

"Would it be possible for us to leave the artifact in your care for the moment?" Charles says to Oldhouse."

"Yes, you can trust us to keep it safe. And we can arrange for a get-together with our Italian friends."

"Terrific," Charles says. "Er, I mean . . . brilliant."

❖

On Wednesday afternoon, while Charles is off doing his usual stint with manuscripts in the Bodleian Library, Allie stakes out a corner of Mrs. Hawkins' garden. She plans to take advantage of the nice day to do some painting. She gets herself organized and an hour later she's well along on a gouache painting she's decided to make in the manner of J.M.W. Turner. She's familiar with several of his garden paintings and feels confident she can produce something similar.

While she paints, the jaunty little tune of "In an English Country Garden" runs through her head. Allie is hardly a traditionalist when it comes to her own original paintings, but she also likes to regularly set herself to make paintings in the style of famous artists, partly because it amuses her, but even more so as a way to stretch herself and maintain her artistic flexibility. She likes to think of it as analogous to athletes doing cross-training. Her father, semi-jokingly, tells her she could earn far more money as an art forger than she ever will as an original artist. Such remarks, however, do not amuse her.

A few hours earlier, around mid-morning, Mrs. Hawkins and her dog Agnes had climbed into Mrs. H.'s ancient Morris Minor station wagon and hit the road for Bournemouth. Mrs. H. would be spending the next week there with her elder sister who had been a bit under the weather. Charles and Allie would mind things here while she was gone, and since she'd taken her dog Agnes with her, there would be no dog-walking this weekend for Peter after all. With Mrs. H. off to Bournemouth and Charles doing his thing in the library, Allie had the house and garden all to herself on this splendid afternoon.

It's along about three when Allie hears footsteps coming up the gravel drive. Has Charles returned earlier than usual? She doesn't expect him until around five-thirty.

Tucked away as she is behind a large shrubbery, Allie isn't actually visible unless someone were to enter the garden and take a peek behind the shrubbery. Allie peers through a small opening and sees a man she doesn't know glancing up at the windows of Charlie's flat. He's a tall slender fellow whose hair is cut unusually short. The man walks to the lower-level entrance, then stops and glances about. He doesn't ring the bell. He reaches out and tries the door handle, which Allie knows is locked. Allie looks down and sees the door keys and her mobile phone lying on top of her handbag.

The man takes a few steps to the left and tries to peer into the kitchen window. He holds a hand up to shield his eyes from the glare of the sun. Then he steps back from the door and looks up again at the upstairs windows of Charlie's flat. Quickly he swings around and glances furtively about him. Is the man thinking about trying to break in? After a few more seconds, he moves back over to the door and tries it again, this time pushing at the handle more forcefully than before. It doesn't budge.

Allie, frozen behind her shrubbery, hopes she's invisible. But now the man turns and stares intently toward the garden. He takes a couple of steps in her direction, then stops to listen. She hasn't made any noise, has she? Now through the small opening in the thick shrubbery Allie can see the man's face. He seems to her an ugly brute, with small black eyes, a protruding nose, and close-cropped hair that makes his sharply pointed ears look like a pair of small bat wings.

The man takes a couple steps and is now standing just outside the open gate to the garden. Oh, god, Allie thinks, the bastard's coming for me.

As the man reaches the garden gate, he pauses. More steps now make crunching sounds on the gravel walkway. Hearing them, the man freezes. Allie hears them, too. Could it be Charlie?

The man swings about to see who it is. It isn't Charlie. It's the postman.

Seeing a fellow he doesn't recognize standing near the

entrance to the garden, the postman says, "'Ullo, 'ullo. You lookin' for Mrs. 'awkins, then?"

The man grunts back something inaudible.

"I reckon she's out walkin' her Dalmatian. Usually does 'bout this time o' day." He shoves a few letters through the mail slot in the front door. "You'll probably have better luck findin' her in an hour or so, eh?"

The man doesn't say anything but nods his understanding. The postman heads back toward the street, but then he pauses there and looks back at the house.

After a long moment of standing there, the stranger begins to move down the drive toward the street. Now that he's been seen, perhaps he thinks he'd better make himself scarce.

Allie is trembling. This is the first time, she realizes, that she's felt real fear since she saw the body laid out on the floor of the church in Glastonbury. Now she can hardly move. She just stands there, hugging herself tightly with her arms. Finally, she stops shaking. She begins to collect her things, knowing there's no chance of getting herself back into the skin of J.M.W. Turner. What a shame. Her little painting had been going so well.

Now Allie hears more crunching sounds on the drive. Bloody hell, what now, she thinks. Is that vile fellow returning?

Allie peeks cautiously around the shrubbery. It's not the vile fellow, it's Charlie! Where the hell have you been, you bastard! she screams inside her head.

"Allie, is everything okay?" Charles calls out, seeing her wild-looking eyes and the paleness of her face.

"Well, I guess it is *now*," she says. "So, Charlie, why don't you come give me a hand with my equipment? But first, why don't you come here and just hold me for a moment."

CHAPTER 21
— The Dreaming Spires —

The soccer game on Thursday isn't the epic struggle of the previous week. Nor do Peter and Dickie reprise their heroics of the earlier game. This time it's their goalie who's the star. With cat-like agility and quickness, he stops every single shot on-goal. Peter's side ends up eking out a 1-nil win.

"Nice for the lads to spread the glory around," Dickie's father says, obviously disappointed that his son wasn't the hero of the day. "Very much a team win today, wasn't it?"

"In American baseball there's nothing I love more than a great pitcher's duel," Charles says. "Today's game was a bit like that."

"Well, *that* I wouldn't know," the man says.

❖

Somehow, George Harpole has managed to get through his Thursday afternoon classes. Now he's set off on the fifteen-minute walk back to his flat. Today, for some reason, his wandering steps take him on a route that goes past the museum where he first met Nadja. If he were to go in, would he find her sitting there behind the information desk like he did before? Of course not. As much as he doesn't want to, George knows he must face the fact that Nadja is dead. He wishes it weren't so, but he knows it is.

Still, for some reason he doesn't understand, George finds himself turning and going inside the building.

Goodness, there *is* a young woman seated at the information desk, and she's seated right where he'd first seen Nadja. Is it Nadja? Of course, it isn't. But George is startled to see how much she resembles Nadja, with her dark eyes, square shoulders, and slim torso.

The young woman looks up and smiles at George. "Can I help you, sir?" she says, her words revealing a slight Eastern European accent.

"Hello," George says. "I'm George. I teach at the university. I love museums. I love *this* museum."

"Hello," she says. "I'm Elena. I'm new to the museum. I just started here last week."

"Welcome to Hull," George says. For five minutes he engages her in conversation. She tells him about a new exhibition that she says will be going up next week. Elena is friendly and has a warm smile, not to mention being very attractive.

"Well, I'd best be off," George says. "I've enjoyed our little chat. Thank you for talking with me."

"Oh, sir, any time. And I hope you will be able to come to the exhibition next week."

George thinks about this young woman named Elena all the way home. He'll definitely attend the exhibition next week. In fact, maybe he'll just pop into the museum tomorrow to chat with her some more. The idea pleases him a great deal.

❖

On the late-afternoon drive from Dorset to Oxford, Peter is unusually chatty, probably because he's so excited about the coming weekend. "Will I be able to go inside the Bodleian Library?" he asks.

"To some parts of it," Charles says. "The professor has special privileges that aren't available to the general public, or even to me. He'll show you all around his college, too, one of Oxford's finest. Maybe he'll trot you about through a couple of Oxford's most famous museums.

As they approach Oxford, Allie turns off the main road onto a narrow lane that leads up Boars Hill. She stops about halfway up the hill. The last rays of the westering sun are just now fully illuminating the Oxford skyline. Neither Charles nor Allie say anything. Words aren't necessary.

Peter drinks in the sight. It's similar to ones of Oxford he's seen in books and on calendars. "It's magical," he whispers.

"The Dreaming Spires," Allie said. "It really requires a telephoto lens to see it properly like what you see on the postcards. But it's still pretty nice, isn't it? Even my father, who hated most things about Oxford, always spoke wistfully of this view of the city. My daddy does his best to present a crusty veneer, but he can be a real softy sometimes, you know?"

"I agree," Charles says. "He's not the curmudgeon he tries to pass himself off as. When he learned of the death of his old Oxford friend, that clergyman we tried to track down in North Cornwall, his grief was palpable."

"Neville Smallwood," Allie says. "Daddy really cared for Neville, just as he really cares for Professor Wentworth."

"Yes," Charles says. "Your father has three great loves—his two old Oxford friends, his spunky and independent-minded daughter, and ancient books. And any man who loves his closest friends, his daughter, and his books, can't be all bad."

Peter smiles at their words, though he doesn't fully understand what they are talking about.

"Thank you so much for bringing me here. Do you mind if I take a photo?" Peter steps from the car. With his cell phone, he takes several shots of the Dreaming Spires. He gets them in just before the fading of the light.

"We thought we'd eat out tonight, Peter," Allie says. "Do you like Indian? Tikka masala or chicken vindaloo?"

"Vindaloo? Oh, miss, vindaloo would be much too spicy for me! Madras is more my level."

"A wise choice, Peter," Charles says. "Allie always tries to push us to the limit."

"But miss, Indian is one of my favorites. That sounds great."

"Indian it is," she replies.

Before going to dinner they take a leisurely drive through the center of the city, down the Broad Street past Blackwell's bookstore on the left side and the heads of the Roman emperors on the right. They pass beneath the Oxford version of the Bridge of Sighs, just across from the Bodleian Library. "The Professor will enjoy walking you about tomorrow," Charles said. "There's nothing he loves more than showing off his beloved Oxford, where he's lived for the last fifty years."

"I'm really looking forward to it too," Peter says. "The

professor is a brilliant man, and a very nice one, too."

They wind down narrow New College Lane until it connects with High Street, then pass on down the High to Magdalen Bridge. When they reach the point where the roads diverge, they swing about and move back up the High passing the Botanic Gardens on their left and Magdalen College on the right. "You'll want to have a good look at the gargoyles you see up there gracing Magdalen College when you're out walking with the professor tomorrow," Charles says. "Take a few photos of some of the niftier ones."

"I surely will, sir."

As they pass St. Mary's Church, Allie says, "Be sure the professor takes you up to the top of the church. You'll be able to experience one of the best of the Dreaming Spires up close, not to mention having one of the finest views of Oxford City in its entirety."

When they reach Carfax, Allie turns left onto St. Aldates. Charles points out Tom Tower gracing the entrance to Christ Church College. Allie points out the Alice Shop a bit farther down on the right.

"Have you read Lewis Carroll?" she asks Peter.

"Actually, I have," he says. "Very droll." His remark causes Charles to laugh.

They find Jamal's, the Indian restaurant in Jericho where they have reservations. The place is packed, but Allie had the forethought to book a table for eight o'clock.

When Allie offers Peter some of her chicken vindaloo, he gamely gives it a try, but it's still well beyond the tolerance of his taste buds. A bite of Charles's spicy curry dish is more to his liking. But he says the chicken tikka masala he ordered for himself is just right.

Back at Charles' flat, they watch an episode of "Inspector Morse" that Charles has on DVD. Then Peter beds down on the sofa and they call it a night.

❖

Professor Wentworth, with an audible sigh, lowers himself onto the wooden bench. "You've worn me out, Peter. I'm plumb tuckered, as they say in those old western movies. Need to rest these old bones for a bit. You go on ahead and explore. That's a lovely stretch of woods in there along the river. Have yourself a good wander but do be careful along the river's edge. It can get quite slippery close up."

"Back in fifteen or twenty minutes, sir. And yes, I shall be careful."

Peter disappears among the trees. They get thicker as he nears the banks of the Cherwell. Now he can hear plashing made by the poles or paddles of folks punting on the river, but there seems to be no one else around. Aside from a few wood pigeons, Peter has the woods to himself. As the sound of punters moves away, he hears only the wood pigeons and a flock of crows atop one of the trees.

A path runs parallel to the river's edge, and Peter moves carefully along it for a few minutes. Now he finds himself in an especially dense, almost desolate-seeming, part of the woods.

Suddenly the boy stops and stands stock still. Has he heard something besides birds? Is someone else here? Has someone been watching him?

Peter strains his ears. He hears only the sounds made by the rustling leaves and his own breathing. It's a bit spooky out here all alone in the shadows of these ancient oak trees. Maybe, he thinks, it's time he should be heading back.

Then, out of the corner of his eye, Peter senses movement. Has someone just slipped behind the trunk of one of the more massive trees? Now the boy begins to feel some fright. Suddenly the crows rise in a flock from high in a tree—no, Peter thinks, not in a *flock*. It's called a *murder* of crows! Whatever they're called, something has scared them. And me, too.

The boy whirls about and sets off like a streaking greyhound. He rushes along the muddy path beside the river, throwing caution to the wind. A downed limb appears across the path, and Peter stutter-steps, then sails over it. When he lands, his feet slip on damp leaves, and he nearly goes down. Righting himself, he dashes onward. But then a hidden root trips him and he tumbles. The impact nearly knocks the wind out of him, but he's on the ground only for a moment. Then he's on the move again, no harm done, though he did have a good knock. Now he's nearly out of the denser area of the forest. and away from the river the grass under foot is much firmer.

Peter shoots out from a copse of oaks and elms, and now angles across the sward toward where he's left the professor, only a couple of hundred yards away. He maneuvers his body in and out of the last few trees, and then there's the professor, still sitting on the bench. As Peter approaches, he sees that the elderly gent's eyes are closed.

Peter slackens his pace and pulls up near one end of the bench. He bends over and puts his hands on his knees, trying not to pant too loudly beside the still dozing professor. Now he begins to feel just a little bit sheepish, running away from what was probably nothing at all. Just his imagination working overtime. Or, if the movement he thought he'd seen really had been someone, they'd probably meant him no harm.

The professor looks up. "Peter, back already? Well, then, why don't we head over to St. Aldates Street and treat ourselves to an ice cream cone. That sound okay?"

"Sounds perfect, sir. It truly does."

CHAPTER 22
— A Murder of Crows —

In the early hours of Saturday morning, Police Constable Fergus McCulley sets off on his rounds from the Oxford police station. He strolls southward down St. Aldates Street and swings left through an open gateway, then strides along the Broad Walk, the long walkway that borders the north edge of Christ Church Meadow.

It's an unusually quiet Saturday morning. No drunks are sleeping it off on the benches he passes, and it's way too early for tourists to be queuing up for admission to Christ Church College to gawk at one of the spots they'd used in filming the Harry Potter movies.

When he reaches the Merton College playing fields on his left, a few hundred yards along the walkway, the young policeman leaves the Broad Walk and angles off to the right and strides across the grass toward thick woods along the River Cherwell. As he strolls through the Meadow, tendrils of mist curl through the trees. The misty morning hasn't deterred the birds in the Meadow from singing up a storm. The dawn chorus is in full spate—he's no expert, but he recognizes the songs of blackbirds, robins, wrens, and warblers. The sunlight begins peeking in from the east through the trees, presaging another fine April day in Oxford. Indeed, it's such a delightful morning that even the sight of the empty beer bottles and take-away wrappers the Friday night revelers left on the grass doesn't detract from the young policeman's cheerful mood.

As he gets closer to the river, a less usual sight arrests the young policeman's attention. Something has been propped against the thick trunk of one of the largest trees. As he steps closer, he realizes that what he's looking at isn't something *propped* against a tree, it's something that's been *affixed* to the tree. And now as he gets closer, he can see better what it is— it's the body of a person, the body of a nearly naked man. PC McCulley stops and stares at the figure. He can hardly believe his eyes. The man's outstretched arms have been attached to the tree, attached by what looks like spikes, his feet, too. The man wears only his undershorts. And what seizes the young constable's attention most of all is the ghastly stab wound in the man's right side.

The poor fellow must surely be dead, PC McCulley thinks. Nonetheless, he immediately follows standard procedure, phoning for the EMTs and calling it in to the local police station. He knows that he must secure and protect what's rather obviously a crime scene. And even though it is highly unlikely that he can do anything for the man, he needs to be sure.

Mindful of not wanting to disturb anything before the forensics folks arrive, he hesitantly steps carefully forward, reaches out and puts one finger against the man's thigh. It's cold to the touch, confirming what he was already pretty sure of. Suddenly, before the young policeman can prevent it, his own body has an involuntary reaction of its own; fortunately, he manages to get several steps away from the dead man before tossing his breakfast of toast, eggs, and coffee. He knows he'll catch some serious grief for having done that. When he feels a second wave of nausea sweeping over him, he struggles to fight it back down.

PC McCulley extracts a hanky from his hip pocket and mops his mouth and face. He struggles to collect himself. When he finally hears the see-sawing sounds of the emergency vehicles' sirens, he sighs in relief. This horrifying experience is far beyond anything the young man has ever experienced.

His phone rings.

"Oh, yes sir, in Christ Church Meadow, while doing my morning rounds. I'm afraid it's a possible homicide, sir," he informs his superior. "No, sir, I've tried to avoid touching anything. I hear the vehicles coming now, sir. No, I haven't identified the man. He's mostly unclothed, so I doubt if there's anything on him to tell us who he is, no wallet or anything.

"No, sir, he doesn't appear to be an undergraduate. He looks at least middle-aged, if not older. Now I think about it, I may have seen this man recently, maybe in the newspapers. Now I have it. Sir, I'm fairly certain he's a professor at one of the colleges. Maybe even a well-known one."

❖

Charles is in the little kitchen of his flat brewing coffee and heating up leftover scones. It's 8:30 on Saturday morning. He's listening to Radio 2, the volume turned low, when a sleepy-eyed lad comes wandering in.

"Morning, sir. What's that you've got on the radio?"

"Morning, Peter. It's Schubert's 3rd, a particular favorite of mine."

"I've heard some Schubert, though mostly shorter pieces. My sister's played some for me. My mum and dad, I'm afraid, aren't so big on classical music."

"Lots of folks aren't. No shame in that, but . . ."

"But it's their loss," the boy says, finishing Charles' thought with a grin.

Allie appears through the kitchen door.

"Smelled the coffee, did you? I must say, you're looking a bit needful," Charles says.

"Oh, you better believe it." Then, holding out her cupped hand she says, "Please, sir, could I have some more?"

"*More!*" Charles says in a loud, gruff voice. Peter is cracking up. "You haven't had any yet, and you already want *more?*"

"Have you read any Dickens?" Allie asks Peter.

"He's on next year's syllabus," Peter says. "But I've seen the *Oliver* movie several times."

Charles pours Allie a cup of his special brew, a combination of Columbian and Sumatran coffee.

"Black or white?" he asks her, knowing she likes to switch around as the mood strikes her.

"Black, please, no sugar."

Peter picks up the cup Charles has poured and hands it to her.

"Oh, thank you, Peter. Today we thought we might drag you about a bit if you're willing. Maybe have a peek at Tolkien's grave, then take a little tour of some of the Oxford places mentioned in the Pullman novels, the places in Will's modern-day Oxford, not those of Lyra's 'alternate world' Oxford."

"That would be grand, miss."

"We don't want to duplicate the things the professor showed you yesterday," Charles says. "Maybe we could take a short walk in Port Meadow along the tow path."

"Along the canal where the Gyptians kept their boats?" Peter asks.

"Oh, well done, Peter," Allie says.

As Allie is getting herself ready, Charles and Peter await her in the flat's sitting room. Spotting the cornet perched on the mantelpiece, Peter says, "Do you play, sir?"

Charles puts the instrument to his lips and proceeds to blow "Reveille."

"Oh, that's fab, sir," Peter says, delighted.

Allie comes in and glares at them. "You telling me to hurry it up or something?"

Now Charles is playing "Morning has Broken," and Allie can't keep from singing along.

"Cat Stevens," she says, when Charles has finished.

"Yes, but it's actually a very old Welsh hymn," Charles says.

"We sometimes sing it in chapel," Peter says. "Our boys choir does a smashing rendition of it, too."

"I much prefer it to 'Reveille,'" Allie says.

Charles and Allie and Peter pack in a very full day. Apparently, something big has been going down in the center of the city, for traffic police are diverting traffic from some of the major roads. But Charles and Alley remain oblivious to whatever it as they concentrate on showing Peter a good time.

In the afternoon they enjoy a picnic in Port Meadow and take a long hike along the towpath. Allie and Peter find themselves deep in a discussion of the Pullman novels. Charles, who has read the novels also and much enjoyed them, chooses just to listen in and follow their impressive discussion. Peter is especially fascinated by Pullman's concept of the people in Lyra's world having a *daemon*, a kind of external soul. He loves Pan, Lyra's daemon. Allie praises the great variety of characters, though in particular she loves a character named Lee Scoresby. She says she considers his death scene in the second book in the series to be one of the most heart-shattering scenes she's ever read. Charles knows the scene she's talking about. He, too, found it poignant and powerful.

It's late afternoon when they finally decide to head back to the flat in North Oxford. Allie suggests they just order a couple of pizzas for dinner, making things easy for them. Peter endorses the idea enthusiastically, as does Charles.

CHAPTER 23
— Sapientia et Fortitudo —

After their meal, the three of them have some down time. Charles spends a few minutes checking on things in Mrs. H.'s downstairs part of the house. He makes sure everything is locked and secured for the night.

When he comes back up to the flat, he pauses a moment in the doorway to the sitting room to look at the two people in the room, two people for whom he has deep affection. There's Peter, sunk down into the comfortable chair near the window, the boy engrossed in the most recent Pullman novel. And there's Allie, sitting on the sofa with her legs curled up beneath her, a faraway look on her face. As he's watching her, she looks up and smiles at him. Her warm smile causes his heart to skip a beat.

Charles comes into the room and moves across to the front window where he stands and looks out. It's not fully dark yet but soon will be. Charles is staring at the twilit-sky when, out of the corner of his eye, he senses movement down on the driveway. He can just make out two dark shapes—a pair of men—and they're heading straight toward Mrs. H.'s front door.

There's no sound of anyone ringing the doorbell or

knocking. That's not a good sign. Charles knows for certain the downstairs front door is securely locked and bolted for he's just checked on that. Nonetheless, it's only a moment later that he hears the telltale squeak the outside door makes when it swings open. How did they do that? he wonders.

Allie and Peter, sensing Charles' unease, both look up at him questioningly. When Charles raises a finger to his lips, Allie and Peter give him nods of understanding.

Soft footfalls can be heard ascending the stairsteps to the upstairs flat. Whoever it is, they are now on the landing. Now they're standing just outside the flat's door.

Charles hears the faint jingle of a key chain. The guy might have a skeleton key, Charles thinks. If so, it won't work, because the door is securely latched from the inside.

No voices, no whispers, no sound at all. Then there comes a metallic scraping against the lock. Suddenly, the inside latch springs back.

Charles sees the door handle begin to turn. He steps forward as quietly as he can and he leans his full weight of 180 pounds against the door. *Wham.* The door bursts open, and Charles is knocked flat on his back. Before he can scramble to his feet, the men are inside the room. One of them rushes at Peter and puts his hands on the boy. The other has grabbed ahold of Allie.

A burly fellow has a chokehold on Peter. His companion clutches Allie, holding a knife against her throat. He has a grin on his ferret-like face.

Charles, who's climbed back to his feet, stands close to the mantelpiece. Peter and the thickset man holding him are over by the window. Allie and the man with the knife snugged against her throat stand in front of the sofa. For a long moment there's a silent tableau as everyone remains just as they are, staring at each other.

Finally, the man with the knife says, "Just give it to us, eh? Give it to us and we'll go. We'll go and leave you in peace. No one will get hurt." In peace? More likely in pieces, Charles thinks, as he sees the man press the knife even more tightly against Allie's throat.

"My wallet's on the mantelpiece," Charles says. "It has my credit cards and a small amount of cash. There's nothing else of value in the flat. Just my laptop computer. You're welcome to that, too."

"Not cash, not cards, not no lousy laptop, wanker. What we want's the bloody artifact that you bastards stole from us. Get the bloody thing now and we won't hurt you. Don't, and it'll be your friends who'll be getting' bloody." He cracks a smile like he thinks he's said something witty.

"We don't have it," Allie says. "It's at the museum. We gave it to them for safe-keeping."

"Liar!" the man screams. "We *know* you didn't. You think we haven't been *watching* you? You think we're *stupid?*" To Charles, the man sounds psychotic.

Charles struggles to reach a decision. The man really sounds like a psycho, and there's one thing Charles knows for certain—he's not going to take any risks with Allie or Peter. Not for the sake of some inanimate object, never mind how valuable it may be or how *holy* it may be. It's a *thing*, Charles thinks, merely a *thing*. The lives of these people he loves are way more important than some inanimate thing.

"Okay," he says, "you win. I do have it. I've got it hidden away behind the mantelpiece. It'll take me a sec to get the thing opened up. Just hang on, okay?"

"Then get on with it," Ferret-face says. "My knife hand's gettin' weary. Could be slipping at any moment now. That wouldn't be so good for this cute little bint, would it now?"

"Charlie, don't give it to them!" Allie cries out.

"You shut your gob, lady," Ferret-face says.

The man holding Peter has been paying close attention to this exchange. Too close, as it turns out, because without realizing it, he's loosened his grip on the boy.

With the agility of a young eel, Peter suddenly twists himself free of the man's grip. Peter's writhing movements and the thickset man's attempts to recapture him distract the man who's got Allie. Suddenly she grabs the wrist of the arm holding the knife against her throat. At the same time, she brings her heel back hard into the man's shin.

In the blink of an eye, Charles snatches the cricket bat from atop the mantel. In the next blink of an eye the bat comes crashing down onto the head of the man with the knife. The rotter drops the knife and crumples onto the carpet.

The burly fellow abandons Peter and lunges at Charles. He pulls a cosh from his pocket, raises it over his head, and takes a vicious swing at Charles. Charles just barely sidesteps the blow and the man's momentum nearly causes him to topple. As he's trying to regain his balance, Charles Bascombe, like Joltin' Joe himself, takes a hard level cut with the cricket bat and brings it straight into the man's mid-section. When the man doubles over in pain, Charles delivers the coup de grâce against the man's skull. *Crack.* The man and the cricket bat are both goners.

Charles still grips one piece of the cricket bat. The other lies on the carpet beside the unconscious man.

Charles, Peter, and Allie stand there panting. They look at each other feeling stunned and confused. Charles notices that Peter is bouncing from foot to foot, no doubt high on adrenaline.

"What did we just do?" Allie says at last. She sounds somewhat bewildered. For a moment no one responds.

"Defended ourselves," Peter finally says. "We defended ourselves."

"Yes," Charles says. "That's what we did. They attacked us and we defended ourselves."

"They were the bad guys," Peter says, "and we did battle with them. The good guys won."

"The good guys did win, Peter," Allie says. "And they couldn't have done it without you." She gives him a big hug.

"I had my doubts about that tatty old cricket bat," the boy says. "Wondered why you'd want to have it. Didn't seem much like a prized possession. Guess I was wrong."

"Better call 999," Allie says. "It would be a good idea to get some reinforcements. Just in case the bad guys aren't entirely finished."

"If they aren't," Peter says, "Mr. Bascombe can deal with them. He wields a wicked bat."

Charles fetches rope from one of the kitchen drawers and

secures the hands and the feet of the still unconscious men. Then, as they await the arrival of the police, their flow of adrenaline begins to ebb.

"The artifact they were seeking," Peter says. "Do you think it could be the same one that I moved in the church, the same one Miss Tremayne found on the lance case and took with her?"

"There's a good chance that it is, Peter," Charles says.

"Were you really going to give it to them?" the boy asks.

Charles rubs his chin. "Discretion is the better part of valor, Peter, so yes, I was."

"Is it really here in the flat?"

"I was wondering that myself, Peter," Allie says. "I didn't think it was. I thought you and the professor left it with the man at the Ashmolean."

"It is at the Ashmolean," Charles says.

"So then how could you give it to them?"

"Like this," Charles says. He reaches behind the mantelpiece and pulls out a small wooden box. He hands it to Peter, who opens it. Peter pulls out an object from a cloth bag and looks at it.

"This is it," he says.

"It is?" Allie asks.

"Looks like it to me," Charles says, with a wink.

"It's a replica!" Allie cries out. "You went and made a replica!"

"Holy moly," Peter says.

"It was the professor's idea. He thought we might want to have a souvenir to take back to America with us."

"So, if Peter hadn't performed his magnificent escape act, you would have given them the replica?"

"That was my plan. It's always possible that they wouldn't have known the difference. Even so, I'm pretty sure it wouldn't have stopped them from, umm, mistreating us, them being the psychos they obviously are."

"Sir, do you think they might have *killed* us?"

Allie gives Charles a warning look.

"Oh, I doubt that," Charles says. "They might have messed us about a bit, but I don't think they would have gone *that* far."

CHAPTER 24

— Ruminations, Reverberations —

George Harpole, as is his habit, leaves his flat on Sunday morning and strolls the half a block to the news agent's where he buys his daily copy of the *Guardian*.

"Mornin', sir," the elderly black man says. The man accepts the five-pound note George hands him, and George waves off the change.

"Much obliged, sir," the man says.

Continuing his Sunday routine, George proceeds to a small coffee shop a couple of doors beyond the newsstand.

At this early hour, he is the only customer. George takes his customary seat at a small table near the front window. The young waitress approaches and says, "Latte, sir?"

"Yes, please, Pippa," George replies with a smile. "And my usual in about ten minutes?"

"Grapefruit juice, wheat toast, marmalade, and a soft-boiled egg?"

"Quite right, my dear, quite right." George admires her trim figure as she turns around and goes to get his coffee. He sighs. Then he thinks of Elena, the woman now working at the museum whose acquaintance he hopes to cultivate. The thought of Elena brings another smile to George's face.

George spreads the newspaper out on the table before him. And then the headline in large bold print smacks him right between the eyes—THIRD CRUXIFICION MURDER. George's empty stomach turns flip-flops. First Nadja, then Geoff, and now an Oxford professor. The man, he learns, is named Martin Nicholson. The name rings a faint bell with George, and then he has it. George had attended a talk given by the fellow just a couple of weeks ago in Glastonbury. My word, George thinks, what a fortunate thing for me that I lost the relic. If I hadn't, maybe that headline would have been about *me* rather than Martin Nicholson. Suddenly his whole body trembles, an icy chill shooting through him. It doesn't cross his mind that if he hadn't lost the artifact, his friend Geoff might still be alive.

As George reads the full account, blood races through his head. Gradually, though, he begins to collect himself. To his great relief, he learns that two suspects are now in police custody. The Oxford don, Martin Nicholson, had been murdered late Friday night or early Saturday morning, and then on Saturday evening, two men had broken into the North Oxford flat of a young American scholar. There, the tables were turned on them. The American and his companions had thwarted the intruders, subdued them, and then held them for the police.

The suspects, according to the article, are Polish nationals. Although little is known about them, it appears they had been in the U.K. for the last few months making the rounds of important museums. The authorities have declined to speculate as to why the Oxford professor was murdered or why the men attempted to break into the American's flat. They think it likely, though, that the two crimes are related and were perpetrated by the same men. The authorities stress that the American scholar is not suspected of any wrongdoing. Indeed, he and his two unnamed companions are commended for their assistance to the police.

The suspects, who had been armed with a knife and a cosh, were laid low by blows from a cricket bat. They are expected to make full recoveries. The police ask that anyone with information about the two suspects, or any other information that could pertain to the three gruesome murders, come forward at their earliest opportunity.

George sits and sips his latte. Does *he* have pertinent information? Undoubtedly, he does. Should he come forward and assist the authorities with their inquiries? He knows he should. But, he asks himself, would that help Nadja? Would that help Geoff? No, far too late for that. So, what would be the point?

❖

At mid-morning on Sunday, Eva Brooksby and Dennis Adams stand arm in arm just below the National Gallery on the terrace overlooking Trafalgar Square. The square is already packed with noisy children dashing about the fountains and climbing on the backs of the huge lions. Parents and assorted tourists snap photographs.

Lord Nelson, high above on his column, doesn't deign to look down upon the goings-on. "Scanning the horizon for the Spanish fleet," Dennis says. Eva gives his arm an affectionate squeeze. She likes it that what Dennis says is always so predictable. She likes it that he's a solid, reliable fellow, unlike most of the men she's known in Oxford. And she likes it that he's enamored with *her*.

When she saw the headline on the front page of the *Times* a couple of hours earlier, she was badly shaken. Reading about a professor having been murdered in Oxford was horrible by itself, and it was made doubly horrible because the murdered don was someone Eva knew. Her associations with Martin Nicholson hadn't been particularly congenial. But to have been murdered as he was in Christ Church Meadow—what an absolutely appalling, terrifying thing.

Of course, for Eva it brought to mind the horrific scene that she and her friends had come upon in the church in Glastonbury a few weeks earlier, a scene she will never ever forget. At the moment she is extremely glad she's here in London with solid, reliable Dennis and not in Oxford.

❖

Dr. M. Xander, the London physician who along with Peter Saunders attended to the unconscious man in the Glastonbury hotel, wends his way up the path leading to the top of Primrose Hill. Already there are quite a few others there enjoying the sunny Sunday morning. Young couples walk hand-in-hand, children chase each other about, kites are soaring, dogs are off their leashes frolicking.

Sunday is Dr. Xander's one day off. Five days a week he attends to the needs of the affluent Muslim community in which he lives. One day each week he volunteers his services to the free clinic for the poorer Muslims of East London. Sundays are his own and he cherishes his morning walk—whether along Regents Canal, through Regents Park, across the area around Lord's Cricket Ground or his favorite, up Primrose Hill.

Normally, Dr. X.'s companion walks with him, but today he is companionless, which suits his mood. For today he has a lot to think about. The newspaper accounts of the gruesome murder in Oxford have shaken him. He was only slightly acquainted with the slain professor, a man who along with his two companions committed a terrible sacrilege by making a replica of a spear revered by Muslims. Dr. Xander had pleaded with the men not to do that. He'd told them that for Muslims that particular spear, used by Muslim warriors during the Third Crusade, was imbued with sacred associations, and thus it was forbidden to reproduce it in any way. Doing that would be a serious desecration of it.

He had warned them. He had appealed to them to respect the tenets of another's religious faith. They'd ignored his pleas. Now, Dr. Xander can't help wondering if this man's ill-advised actions engendered his own demise?

Dr. Xander is a physician, first and foremost. He can never continence one human being taking the life of another. And so, he cannot condone what happened in Oxford. But he knows, too, he'll never fully understand the workings of the divine mind.

❖

At mid-morning on Tuesday, Albert and Edwin enter Oxford's busy Covered Market from one of the entrances on High Street. It takes them just a moment to locate Brown's Café, where Professor Wentworth suggested the three of them might meet for coffee and a chat.

Brown's is a venerable Oxford establishment with a homey atmosphere. Today, like most days, its tables are occupied primarily by students and professors. They spot Professor Wentworth in a far corner where he's commandeered a table, his hat atop one chair, his jacket draped over the back of another.

"Greetings, Professor," Edwin says, lifting a hand.

"Grab yourselves a seat, my friends," the professor says. The two men do.

At a table nearby a pair of undergraduates are debating vociferously. Their bone of contention is the novels of Martin Amis. "Bloody brilliant," the young man avers, "even better than Rushdie."

"Overrated, pretentious crap," the young woman declares, slapping one hand hard against the table top.

Albert, sotto voce, says, "I'm with her." Edwin, who hasn't read a novel since *King Solomon's Mines* when he was twelve, gives a noncommittal shoulder shrug. The professor makes a little head wag, then says, "people more knowledgeable than I rate Amis's work highly. I tried them. Not quite my cup of tea."

"Pretentious crap," Albert says loudly repeating the young woman's words. The students glance in the direction of the older men, the young woman grinning.

"I bow to your erudition," Edwin says with a straight face.

"Anyway, Professor," Albert says, "we appreciate your willingness to give us a few minutes of your time. We have just a few questions for you, then you can get back to your musty old manuscripts or whatever."

"Then fire away."

"First off, how well did you know Martin Nicholson?"

"Not well. Our fields overlap, so we crossed paths now and then at meetings, talks, or the odd social event. Don't think we ever exchanged more than a few casual remarks. He and I tended to move in different social and intellectual circles."

"You aren't suggesting that his scholarship was somewhat, um, second rate?"

"Certainly not. Published in some top journals. The topics just weren't . . . of particular interest to me."

"I think the professor is choosing not to speak ill of the recently deceased," Edwin says.

"Did you hear his talk in Glastonbury?" Albert asks.

"No, actually, I had a nap. Early start for me that day."

"Any idea why those blokes would have targeted him particularly?" Edwin asks.

"Not really. Maybe they thought he was holding out on them."

"Holding out?"

"Might've thought he knew where the artifact was but wouldn't tell 'em."

"And what do you suppose Nicholson's connection with the artifact could have been?" Albert asks.

"Don't know. Charlie and Allie think he was involved in some sort of conspiracy with Nigel Bright-Rogers and MacPherson, his Scottish pal. Seems they overheard the three of them having a curious conversation one night in Glastonbury."

"Maybe they might've figured that of the three of them he

was the weakest link?" Edwin suggests.

"And his being here in Oxford made him the easiest one to come after," Albert says.

They pause to sip their coffee. The two undergraduates rise from their table and shoulder their backpacks, casting quick glances at the three older men as they depart. The young man mutters, "Old geezer doesn't know shit about good literature."

Albert hears the remark, as intended, but refrains from firing back a vulgar comment of his own. The professor finishes a last bite of croissant, and the waitress comes over and tops up their coffee mugs. "Thank you, Margaret," the professor says to her.

"Margaret?" Albert asks, grinning. Then he says, "'Margaret are you grieving over Goldengrove unleaving?'" Edwin rolls his eyes.

"Ah," the professor says, "Hopkins. Unusual poet."

"*Anyway*," Edwin says, sounding a bit irritated by the other two men's intrusive nonsense, "to return to the matter at hand . . . one might say that those fellows seem to have a flair for the dramatic, *crucifying* their victims. Why do you suppose they kept on doing that?"

The professor tilts his head and lifts his shoulders in a shrug.

"Well, maybe just psychos and masochists," Albert says. "But the artifact they were seeking, Professor. Do you have any idea what it is? And do you have any idea what might have happened to it and where it might be now?"

The professor purses his lips and rubs the back of one hand across his chin. At last he says, "The answer to both your questions is—maybe."

"Kindly elucidate," Albert says.

"Quite possibly, it is a unique and very holy relic, one that holds great importance to Christians. If it is, it would be extremely valuable—which is why, I suspect, some people would be willing to commit murder in the effort to obtain it."

"A very holy relic? Could you be more specific, Professor?" Edwin asks.

"Oh, come now," the professor snaps. "What spear tip could possibly hold such great importance to Christians?"

"Only one I can think of," says Albert. The professor tilts his head noncommittally.

"Then," says Edwin, "where do you think it might be? Any idea?"

"I don't know where it is at the moment, but I have an idea where it could eventually end up."

"And where's that?" Ewin asks.

"Where it belongs," the professor says simply. The two men look at him, silently urging him to continue. "And that, of course, would be on the end of the lance from whence it came."

❖

The room is dim, and it requires an effort for Peter Saunders to pry his eyes open. Predawn light is just creeping through the window into his small room in The Knoll, his school residence hall.

Peter feels immense relief—at being awake and being alive. The morning's light has rescued him from another horrific dream, for it isn't the first time his subconscious mind has provided a different ending to those traumatic events in Oxford a month ago. At the time, Peter's conscious mind hadn't registered how close he and Miss Tremayne and Mr. Bascombe had come to being killed in Mr. Bascombe's flat. But for the last several weeks his subconscious has insisted on sending him a different message. Yes, Peter has to acknowledge, those two fellows who forced themselves into the flat really could have done them in, had events gone differently.

But—they hadn't. Peter, Charles and Alwyn, acting in concert, had thwarted their attackers and taken them down. They were heroes—and Peter had played a part in all of it.

"So, listen here, you foxy little demon," Peter says to his subconscious mind, "it's time for you to just *bugger off!*"

CHAPTER 25
— Pennies from Heaven —

It's a Sunday afternoon early in the month of May, and Albert and Edwin stroll through North Oxford's Summertown. They're on their way to Charles' flat, intending to make an unannounced visit to Charles and Allie.

"You realize we owe those two young folks quite a debt of gratitude," Albert says.

"Oh yes, we surely do," Edwin replies. "Did a large share of the heavy lifting for us, those two did. Showed a lot of intelligence and courage in the process."

"*Sapientia et fortitudo*, the two great Anglo-Saxon virtues," Albert says, "like Beowulf and Frodo, and all those fellows."

"No reason why an American can't have Anglo-Saxon virtues," Edwin says.

"Or a plucky young Cornishwoman. She has guts and gump-tion, does Alwyn Tremayne," Albert says.

"Brains and courage."

"Yes," Albert says. "And some nice curves as well.'

"You noticed, eh?" says Bert."

A few minutes later the two men stand on the landing outside the door to Charles' flat. Edwin gives the door a gentle rap. After a beat, Charles opens it, a wide grin appearing on his face. Allie is standing just behind him.

"Allie, look who's here," Charles says. "It's Bert and Ernie, my two favorite . . . what-ever-you-ares."

"Retirees," Albert says.

"Retirees, hah," Allie says.

"Well, whatever you are, do come in?" Charles says. "Come and set yourselves down. Would you like something to drink?"

"No, no, I'm fine," Albert says. Edwin nods to say he is, too.

"Actually, this is slightly more than just a social call," Albert says.

"Oh, yes?" Allie says. "After all this time, it's finally dawned on you that Charlie and I are nothing but a pair of vile thieves and murderers?"

Albert laughs. "Oh, my dear, nothing at all like that. You may have perfected the art of prevarication, but you certainly are not thieves and murderers."

"Prevaricators?" Allie says. "You have the audacity to suggest that your fellow cribbage players are prevaricators?"

"Well, why don't we get right to it," Albert says. "So, sir and miss, if you don't mind my asking—the spear point? Could you tell us where it has ended up?"

"The holy relic those guys who busted in here were looking for?"

"That would be the one," says Edwin.

"You mean you don't know?" Charles replies.

"I could hazard a guess,"Albert says, "but why don't you tell me?"

"Do you see that little box on the mantel piece?" Charles says, pointing.

"That's it? You still have it?" Edwin asks, incredulously.

"Why don't you take a look?" Allie says.

Edwin opens the box and extracts the spear point. "Well, I'll be blowed!" he exclaims, then hands it to Albert.

"Only one problem," Albert says, examining it. "This isn't it, is it? Here you go prevaricating again."

"Are you sure this isn't it?" Charles asks.

"No, but logic decrees that you've long since parted with the thing."

"And so does a look at Allie's financial records," Edwin adds.

"My financial records!"

"Yes, we're embarrassed to admit that we needed to have a look," Albert says.

"So, how much remuneration did you actually receive?" Edwin asks.

"Remuneration? Us? Poor as church mice we were, and poor as church mice we still are."

"And yet a good bit of money seems to have passed through your hands. Donation to the Pitt-Rivers Museum, donation to the Ashmolean Museum, and a trust fund for that young man named Peter Saunders, the lad we saw on the tape going into the church in Glastonbury, the lad who was with you the night you apprehended those foul murderers."

"Peter's worth far more than the modest amount we put into the trust fund for him. We're just hoping it will be enough to ensure he gets a proper university education."

"A laudable intention," Albert says.

"Indubitably," Allie replies.

"Miss," Edwin askes, "could you explain the donations to the museums?"

"Appropriate compensation for the kind assistance they rendered us. Nothing more than that."

Albert nods. "Seems reasonable to me," he says. He looks down and realizes he's still holding the fake relic. "And what were you planning to do with this one? Just keep it as a happy reminder?"

"That was our intention," Charles replies. "But now I have another idea."

"And what is that?" Edwin asks.

"We thought we might just send it to a museum in Manchester. They could add it to the replica they already have of the spear in the Vatican."

"It was our impression," Edwin says, "that you weren't too keen on that fellow Nigel Bright-Rogers. Considered him to be a rather slippery sort of bugger—if you'll pardon my French."

"Slippery indeed," Charles says. "Bright-Rogers actually offered to buy the artifact from us for 450,000 euros."

"Cheap bastard," Albert says. "He would have collected five times that amount from the folks at the Vatican," Albert says.

"My words exactly," Allie says. "But if it wasn't for him and MacPherson, there would have been no exhibition of the lance replicas, in which case the atifact would never have fallen into our hands."

"*Fallen* into our hands," Charles says with a laugh. "Inter-esting way to put it."

"And," Allie goes on, ignoring Charles' remark, "we applaud Bright-Rogers for displaying all the replicas in his new museum. That's a worthwhile endeavor in itself."

"This artifact," Albert says, "I take it you know what the thing really is and why so many people have been so desperate to get their hands on it?"

"Why it's so valuable people are willing to kill to get it?" Edwin adds, with a questioning tilt of his head.

"We know what it *might* be," Charles says. "The experts at the Pitt-Rivers dated it to the First Century B.C., Roman, in all probability."

"But would such an object possess immense value?" Edwin asks, eyebrows arched. "Seems unlikely to me. Roman spear points aren't all *that* rare."

"It would if it could be confidently associated with an immensely important historical event," Allie says.

"Like the death of Mark Antony or Cleopatra. Something like that?" Albert asks.

"Yes . . . ," Allie says, "something like that."

"But miss," Edwin says, "where did all that money come from? One moment your bank account is practically empty and the next you are handing out charitable gifts like there's no there's no tomorrow. Would you mind enlightening us on that point?"

Allie looks at Charlie, but as usual, he's no help at all. He shrugs his shoulders and turns his palms outward.

"Where did all the money come from? Well," Allie says, "I suppose you could say it was pennies from heaven."

"That would be one big boatload of pennies," Edwin says.

"And," Albert says, "if the money did come in a metaphorical boat, perhaps it came from somewhere like . . . Italy? But knowing you two, I'm guessing that try as we might, we'll never be able to get the full story out of you."

"Sir, I swear to you," Allie says, "I have never in my life told you a single untruth."

"No," Edwin says, "you've just conveniently skipped over things, as is your wont. Prevarication by omission."

"And that, sir, comes from a man who passes himself off as a retiree."

Albert laughs, then so does Edwin. "You got me there," he says.

For the last couple of minutes Edwin has been eyeing the cribbage board he's spotted lying on the mantelpiece. He steps over and picks it up.

"This one's a classic," he says to Charles. "My old father had one just like it."

"Like to buy it?" Charles says. "I'll make you a heck of a deal."

"No, I'll pass on buying it. But how about we use it for its intended purpose, if you happen to have a deck of cards."

"I think we might just be able to track down a deck. And Charlie, we have just enough time for a game before our evening plans, right?" Allie says. She looks at Charles who nods.

"This time around," Albert says, "why don't we try switching things up a bit. Alwyn, why don't you play with me, and Edwin with Charles?"

"No way, José," Allie says firmly. "Charlie's my partner. "

Albert shrugs. "Thought it was worth a try."

"You thought wrong."

"Can't blame a fellow for trying."

Their previous game a month ago in a hotel in Glastonbury, which had been hotly contested, ended up going to Albert and Edwin. This time Allie and Charles peg out, crossing the line first.

"Got ya!" Allie crows.

"Just luck," Albert says.

"Luck, ha! Pure skill," Allie declares.

"Now that we have a game apiece, guess we'll need to play one more to break the tie," Edwin says.

"Can't do it right now," Allie says, "but if you're lucky, maybe we can squeeze one in before we head off for the States."

"So you are going, then?" Albert asks.

"It was the professor who talked me into it. Lectured me about how I needed to broaden my horizons."

"Good advice," Albert says.

"Yes. But I think Charlie might have had something to do with it, too," Edwin says.

"Charlie had a lot to do with it. Our laconic Charlie even told me that he definitely wants me to come with him."

The two men look at Charles.

"Yes, I did say that," Charles says, "I'll admit that I did. I said it because . . . it's absolutely true. I don't want to go back to America unless Allie Tremayne comes with me. And fellas, believe me, for once in my life I am not prevaricating."

—The End —